MIDNIGHT MOON

REBEL WOLF BOOK 1

LINSEY HALL

1

Lyra

"Please, Lyra, I'm begging you." Desperation flashed in Meg's eyes. "Take the end of my shift, and I'll owe you forever."

I stared at my friend, my stomach twisting. "Seriously, Meg? You know I can't afford to lose this job. And I'm not even supposed to be on the top floor."

Meg's eyes dropped to the insignia on the ugly teal maid's uniform I wore, a badge that indicated I was one of the lower-tier maids who worked the bottom floors of the Windracer Hotel.

"No one will notice your badge," Meg said. "Let your hair down. It will cover it."

I raised my hand to my dark hair, which was pulled

back in a boring bun. "You know I can't do that. Boris would have a fit."

Our boss was notoriously picky and mean-spirited. He'd recently fired a girl for having a tattoo that peeked out of the sleeve of her shirt, and another employee for being late.

"Please. Tommy can only get this afternoon off, and I haven't seen him in a week. You can be in and out of the penthouse in no time. *He's* not even there."

The penthouse.

I'd never been on the top floor of the hotel, much less inside the penthouse. But that wasn't the part that got my heart racing—no, it was the mention of *him.*

Garreth Locke, the wealthiest and most dangerous man in Seattle. And handsome, so handsome he could grace the covers of magazines—if he'd ever lower himself to do something so plebeian.

He was young—only five years older than my twenty-four—but my father had spoken of him before he'd died eleven years ago. He'd said that Garreth was the son of another mob boss who ran an organization that rivaled the one my father was involved with. My father had seen Garreth kill a man in cold blood. Apparently, he'd broken the man's neck for deceiving him.

Garreth had been only seventeen at the time. He'd disappeared from Seattle shortly after but returned a few years ago when his father had died.

I shivered at the memory of the story.

Midnight Moon

3

The first time he'd shown up at the hotel, I couldn't believe my eyes. He'd never been caught for what he did. Not surprising. People with that kind of power were seldom punished. I'd caught a glimpse of him a few times as he strode across the lobby, followed by a small group of people nearly as good looking and scary as him. He was more than merely handsome. There was something about him that was otherworldly.

"It won't take you any time at all," Meg said.

I glared at her. This was one of the few decent jobs that paid under the table—thank fates Boris was cheap about paying employee taxes—and I *really* couldn't afford to lose it. But it was rare she asked for anything, and I hated to say no. "Fine, but I'm going to make it quick. I'll do a pretty crappy job, but I'll do it."

"Oh, thank you!" Meg threw her arms around my shoulders and squealed in my ear.

I winced, my ears ringing. My hearing had always been freakishly good, and Meg had the pipes of a banshee.

She pulled back. "I'll make it up to you." She grimaced slightly. "Oh, one more thing. Boris said we're *not* to be in the room when Garreth Locke is there—*no matter what.* So, get in and out."

"What the hell?"

"Sorry, should have mentioned it earlier."

"Should have mentioned that I was *really* risking my

job by doing this for you?" And the last thing I wanted was to be caught by Garreth Locke.

She waved a hand dismissively. "You'll be fine. He's not supposed to be back for hours."

"All right. But if he comes back while I'm in there, I might run for it and leave the housekeeping cart behind."

"Fair enough."

"Good. Now get out of here and go see your boyfriend."

She grinned widely, then spun around and raced out of the breakroom on the bottom floor of the hotel. I sighed and looked up at the clock. I still had a few more rooms on the second floor to clean, but if Garreth Locke wasn't in the penthouse right now, I should go now and get this over with.

Anyway, Boris was supposed to be out to a late lunch. I couldn't afford for him to catch me on the wrong floor, or I risked another mark on my record. One more infraction, and I'd be out on my ass without a job.

Heart pounding, I grabbed Meg's housekeeping cart and hurried to the staff elevator. As it whizzed toward the top floor of the historic hotel, I went over the tasks that I absolutely had to do in the penthouse. The bare minimum—that's what I'd do.

When the elevator opened on the top floor, I peeked out into the entry hall.

Empty.

Thank God.

I hurried toward the penthouse door, careful to keep my face turned away from the security camera. From the back, I looked enough like Meg that no one would think to check twice if they couldn't see my face.

With faintly shaking hands, I used Meg's key card to get into the room. As the door opened, a low chime sounded. Every room in the hotel was equipped with one so guests would know if their door had opened while they were in the bathroom or resting.

The room itself was silent as the grave, and my heart slowed its frantic beating.

"This will be fine," I whispered to myself. "You can do this."

I didn't believe it, but I ignored the warnings screaming at the back of my mind.

The penthouse was a good enough distraction, however. The main room I had entered was large, with enormous floor-to-ceiling windows. They were an older style, installed when the hotel had been built over a hundred years ago, but the long panes of glass still revealed a phenomenal view of Puget Sound and Mount Rainier. The dark water glittered under the light of a rare sun, the snow-capped mountain in the distance standing sentinel.

As quickly as I could, I made my way around the living room. The furniture was simple and luxurious—far nicer than the furnishings on the lower floors of the hotel. And that was saying something, considering those floors contained furniture about ten times nicer than the stuff that decorated my tiny studio in the shit part of town.

I ignored the fabulous view in favor of looking for clues about the life of someone as powerful and dangerous as Garreth Locke. There was nothing, of course. He was tidy as a monk, leaving no indication about his personality or lifestyle.

Most people thought of him as a slightly shady businessman, but I knew differently from my father's stories. He was fully entrenched on the wrong side of the law, and he wouldn't want people to know what he was capable of.

The bedroom was a bit different, the sheets tangled and mussed, as if he'd had awful nightmares. Or excellent sex.

"Get your mind out of the gutter," I muttered, yanking the sheets off the king-size bed.

I remade the lake of smooth cotton as quickly as I could, my gaze snagging on a book that sat on the bedside table. It looked old, really old, and my heart raced.

I *loved* books, and I knew at a glance this one was special.

I arranged the decorative pillows at the head of the bed and picked up the book. I shouldn't do it, but I couldn't help myself.

Just one little peek.

The cover was embossed with flaking golden script —*The History of the Wolves of North America.*

I felt my eyebrows rise. The hardened criminal was an animal person?

That was unexpected.

Gently, I flipped open the cover and revealed the title page. The scent of old paper wafted up, and I inhaled deeply. Before I knew it, I was sucked into a description of various wolf packs that lived around the upper northwest.

I had no idea how much time passed, but the sound of the penthouse door opening made my heart jump into my throat.

He's here.

Triple shit.

He was in the living room. I couldn't see him from the bedroom, but I could feel him. His presence was impossible to miss.

I was screwed.

If only I could wave a magic wand and get myself out of there. Shame that magic wasn't real.

From the living room, he had two options—go into the bathroom or into this bedroom.

Please choose the bathroom.

The bathroom had two doors—one that entered from the living room and one that entered from the bedroom, where I was trapped. I could see right into the bathroom through the cracked door, but if I tucked myself flat against the wall, I'd be mostly concealed by the heavy bed frame.

With any luck, he would go in there, take a shower, and wouldn't turn and see me. Then I could sneak out.

My heart thundered, nearly deafening, as I slipped into my hiding spot.

Garreth

She was here.

My mate.

Inside, my wolf howled.

Down boy.

The beast didn't listen, but I didn't care. There wasn't a chance in hell that I'd release him. Not in the city in the middle of a human hotel. Instead, I stood stock still inside the penthouse living room.

She was in the bedroom. I knew where she was because I could smell her, her scent twisting around me —lavender and honey and a fresh breeze. I wanted to breathe it in for eternity, surround myself with it.

No.

I couldn't be distracted by her. Couldn't let her get under my skin or into my heart. Not that I had a heart.

Protect.

The instinct welled so strongly inside me that I could barely tamp it down.

It was clear as day from her scent that she wasn't a wolf. She was something magical, though I had no idea what.

Why the hell was she in this hotel?

If she was here to confront me, it was a terrible location. The damned place was full of humans. I stayed here when on business purely to make them think I was one of them. They didn't know about magic, and I wasn't going to be the one to let the cat out of the bag. Or rather, the wolf.

The scent of her hit me like a bus. I hadn't expected it—now or ever. As Alpha, I had planned to walk the earth alone, solely dedicated to my pack. I'd been born to this role and kept my status through sheer strength and pack loyalty.

So what the hell *should* I do?

"Take a shower," I muttered to myself.

It was what I'd come here to do, after all I'd worry about her later. Anyway, I wanted to see what she'd do. If she thought my guard was down, she might reveal her true motivations for being in my hotel suite.

I strode into the bathroom, flicking on the light inside the white marble oasis. There were two doors-- one that led back out into the living room from which I'd come, and another that opened into the bedroom.

I made a point not to glance into the bedroom as I stripped my shirt over my head. The cool breeze of the air conditioning wafted over my heated skin but did nothing to tamp down the inferno inside me. My wolf was going mad, demanding to be set free. I kept it on a tight rein. My impeccable control was half the reason I was qualified to be alpha, and I wouldn't allow it to fail me now.

I heard the faint intake of her breath as I walked by the open door, and it took every ounce of my strength not to turn and look at her.

She'd make the first move if I had anything to say about it.

I unbuckled my belt with one hand while cranking on the water. It roared forth, and I couldn't help but look forward to the water pressure. It had been a long day.

As I shucked my trousers, I felt my wolf go wild. He sensed that I was planning to ignore her, and he was *pissed.*

"Tough luck, buddy," I muttered.

I climbed into the shower and turned to face the back wall. The water dampened my hearing, though not completely. She wouldn't be able to sneak up on me. I doubted she'd approach me in the shower, anyway.

Still, anticipation flooded me.

My mate.

After so long alone, so long expecting I would *always* be alone--she was here.

2

Lyra

I stood, stunned, my breath caught in my chest. Sound roared in my head, the crashing of waves on the beach.

His body.

I'd caught a glimpse of him through the cracked door, but that had been enough, providing a too-good-to-be-true view of his back as he stripped out of his shirt.

Holy tits, he was ripped.

My mouth went dry with fear—and even a little bit of desire—as I took in his broad shoulders and smooth skin. He was all muscle and a *lot* of it. I couldn't see his face, but his long dark hair was held back with a leather strap. It shined beneath the light, putting the finest silk to shame. There was the strangest golden glow around him, but that had to be a trick of the light.

But it was his scent that really got me—a divine combination of the forest and rain. I wanted to suck it into my lungs forever. As I stared, the taste of chocolate hit my tongue. He was making me lose my mind.

When he passed by the bathroom door, he somehow didn't turn to look at me. It was a gift. A few precious seconds to figure out what the hell to do.

I need to run.

But I couldn't. I felt trapped, ensnared by his beauty and frozen with fear. It was the strangest sensation and nearly impossible to place.

Until I did.

I felt like prey.

He was ignoring me, and yet I still felt like he was a predator toying with me.

I shivered.

I needed to get my ass out of here, pronto, Meg's warning about not being caught while he was there ringing in my head.

Cold fear iced my skin.

I can't lose this job.

And I really *can't get caught by Garreth Locke.*

More than that, I felt an overwhelming desire to run. It was so strong that I couldn't fight it.

The shower turned on, and I thanked my lucky stars.

Midnight Moon

The sound of the water would give me a little more cover.

I grabbed the cart and pushed it toward the living room, thankful that the wheels were well greased, and it was silent. Every inch of my skin prickled as I approached the bathroom door. I had to pass right by it, and it would be the riskiest part of my escape.

The second door was wide open, and I peeked inside.

Garreth Locke stood in the shower, his back to me as water sluiced over the endless planes of muscles. My gaze raced over his form, quickly taking it all in as I pushed the cart past.

Almost to the door.

When I reached it, I looked out the peephole to make sure the coast was clear.

My stomach plunged. A member of his entourage was approaching the door, along with my boss.

They were coming right in here. I'd be caught.

Panic shot through me. Mind racing, I stumbled back.

The closet.

There was a large closet near the door. I'd seen it when I'd first come in. I yanked open the door and pushed the cart inside. it barely fit, but I managed to shut the door behind it.

With any luck, no one would look inside, and I could

come back later and retrieve it. I'd warned Meg I might leave it behind, but I hated to get her in trouble.

Fast as I could, I raced back to the bedroom where the huge old windows gave a glorious view of the sound.

The prey feeling was so strong inside my chest that I felt like I might pass out at any moment. I wasn't normally such a wimp, but something about this situation seemed to be taking over my body.

I was going to get the hell out of here, no matter what.

Silently, I pushed a window open, thanking my lucky stars that this was an old hotel with normal windows. If I'd been in one of the modern high rises, I'd be screwed.

Cool wind whipped my hair around my face. I ignored the dark strands and climbed out of the window, clinging to the side of the building. I was ten stories up, and the fall would certainly kill me.

Garreth

I stiffened, my preternatural hearing picking up the slight creak of a window opening.

Was that my mate? I strained my ears but couldn't be

sure. I'd heard her run for the hallway door, then scurry back into the bedroom and over to the window.

And now she was leaving? *Through the window?*

Suddenly, this was a hell of a lot more interesting.

Interest piqued, I stepped out of the shower, water dripping onto the marble floor, and walked into the bedroom. The wind caught a flicker of skirt outside the window.

Holy fates, she was scaling the outside of the building.

As I hurried over to the window, the main door to the suite opened. Ignoring the distraction, I pushed the window open and stuck my head out, not wanting to startle her.

Once again, I was too late. All I saw was the flutter of cloth as she turned the corner of the building and disappeared. Curiosity welled so strongly within me that I nearly climbed out to follow her.

Not an option, however. The last thing I needed was to be caught naked, scaling the outside of a human hotel. The street was dead silent below, and there were no boats close enough to see, but with my luck, a tour bus would pass by.

I heard my beta say something to the hotel manager in the other room and snapped back to my senses.

I closed the window. I wasn't even sure I *wanted* to find this woman.

Inside, my wolf howled. *Liar.*

I ignored him and returned to my shower, leaving Seth and the manager to their meeting, knowing I was making the right call.

I was in Seattle preparing to attend the winter gathering, an annual meeting of the leaders of all the shifter packs on the west coast. It would determine the fate of my pack, which was teetering on the brink of collapse after my father's disastrous time as alpha.

Still, it was impossible to get my mind off the woman's scent.

Impossible not to imagine her scaling the outside of the ten-story building.

What *was* she?

3

Lyra

Ten stories below me, the ground beckoned.

Good thing I wasn't going to fall.

I might be a giant nerd, but I was a graceful one. In addition to my weirdly good hearing, I was an excellent climber. As a kid, I'd had a daredevil streak a mile wide. I'd long since squashed it, but the skills still occasionally came in handy.

I clung to the side of the building, adrenaline racing through me as I eased the window back down behind me. If I were being honest with myself, I'd *wanted* to do something dangerous. It felt like years since I had, and the adrenaline rush was glorious.

Quickly as I could, I skirted around to the side of the

building. There was a tiny stone ledge wide enough for my toes, and I was able to find hand holds on the windowsills and brick wall. My heart thundered in my chest, but I freaking *loved* it.

I needed to do this more often.

No, crazy lady.

When I reached the corner of the building, I found myself in the narrow passage of an alleyway, and the fire escape caught my eye. I shimmied over to it, my hands closing around the cold metal railings, and something like disappointment welled in me.

I was having *fun*.

This was way better than cleaning hotel suites.

"But it doesn't pay the bills, dummy. And it certainly won't pay your tuition."

Instead of heading down toward the alley, I climbed toward the roof. It'd be easier to go down, but then I'd have to get back into the hotel at ground level, and someone might see me. and think I was taking an unauthorized break. Better to sneak back through the interior.

Cold wind whipped across my face as I scrambled onto the roof. The view was incredible, the city on one side and the sound on the other. As always, the sight of the water and mountains called to me. Sometimes— hell, always—it felt like I wasn't meant to live in the city at all.

Instead, I was meant to live in the deep forests and

Midnight Moon 19

on the glorious beaches of coastal Washington State. Sadly, that part of the country was lacking in available under-the-table jobs, and I needed this one to pay rent and raise money for school. I'd put my dreams off long enough, and coastal Washington could wait.

I shook the thought away and headed toward the small wooden door that led to the top floor of the hotel. It was an ancient little thing, a relic of the hotel's past.

The door was locked, of course, but that didn't slow me down. I yanked a couple of pins from my hair and got to work on picking the lock. The skills returned quickly, and within seconds, I was inside.

Thank fates for my unsavory past.

I hadn't always been a hotel maid. When I was fourteen and my mother had died of an overdose, I'd made my living as a petty thief. A good one, in fact.

Until my father's old buddies had found me. He'd run with the local mob, and apparently, being a thief put me in their way too often. They'd wanted me to repay his debt, but there was no way I could afford it.

I'd had to quit that gig and get this one. Since I was paid under the table, there was no way for them to find me through their moles at the IRS. The fact that I was applying to the Seattle School of Business was risky, but I sincerely doubted they were checking every school register.

Anyway, I couldn't spend my life cleaning hotel

rooms, and being a thief riddled me with guilt, even though the skills were now coming in handy.

I made my way silently down the stairs toward the top floor of the hotel, then slipped out to the main hallway. Quickly as I could, I headed to the stairs. I didn't want to risk the elevator in case someone was in there.

Silently, I went down the old stairs that twisted around themselves. I was halfway to the bottom when I passed the door that led to the fourth floor.

It opened, and my boss entered.

Shit.

He was supposed to be in the penthouse. What the hell was he doing here already?

His eyes narrowed as he spotted me, and I barely resisted cringing.

"Lyra? What the hell are you doing here?"

"I'm, ah—"

"Hiding away and reading again, were you?" Venom infected his voice. "You really need to be a better team player, Lyra, if you want to keep this job."

Inside, I screamed at the injustice of it all. He'd only caught me reading *on my break,* and I was freaking helping Meg right now, for God's sake.

Instead of telling him that, however, I just nodded. "Of course."

He relaxed, seemingly satisfied, and his gaze moved down the front of my body. Revulsion crawled over my skin, and I whirled and ran down the stairs.

Midnight Moon

"Better get back to work!" I called over my shoulder, desperate to get away from him.

I'd made a point never to be caught alone by him. His eyes creeped me out, and I didn't need to be a mind reader to figure out what he was thinking.

The rest of my shift passed uneventfully, though it felt like my heartbeat never slowed down. I expected Garreth Locke to barge into every room I was working in and demand to know why I'd invaded his space.

He doesn't know you're the one who left the cart.

Fortunately, there was no mention of the cart at all, for which I was grateful. I felt guilty as hell for leaving it, but I was still planning to go back and retrieve it.

Then something miraculous happened.

Meg returned.

"You're kidding me," she said as I told her the whole story in the breakroom. I was finally off shift and had been about to head back up to try my luck at getting the cart back.

"I'll do it," she said. "You've done enough for me. And at least I'm supposed to be up there."

"Oh, thank you." The relief nearly made me collapse. I'd been wound tight with worry over heading back up to the penthouse.

Normally, the excitement of doing something against the rules would get me going, the same way climbing the outside of the building had.

Instead, the memory of Garreth Locke had my heart

going a mile a minute. He wasn't even supposed to be up there, according to Kyle at the front desk, and the thought of him still made my heart race.

"I'm getting out of here." I grabbed the ratty old bag that contained my street clothes and headed toward the staff bathroom.

"Thanks again, Lyra," Meg said. "I owe you one."

"*Several* ones." I grinned at her as I shut the door behind me and pulled off the hated maid's uniform. Boris made us wear the worst costumes, and I wanted to light the damned thing on fire, waving it around my head as I charged out of this hellhole while declaring that I quit.

That wasn't going to happen anytime soon, however. At least I felt like myself as I changed into jeans and an ancient Madonna T-shirt, then tugged on my old boots and swung the battered leather jacket on.

I looped the bag over my shoulder and headed out of the breakroom, toward the back entrance of the hotel. Luck was smiling on me, because I made it out without seeing Boris or any other staff members.

But my good fortune ran out as I tried to start my old motorcycle. The engine sputtered and died at the exact same moment that Ed walked outside. The luggage handler's eyes lit up when he saw me, and I resisted a grimace.

Ed was a nice guy. It wasn't his fault he had the hots for me, and I was thoroughly uninterested in *any* guy.

Midnight Moon

The memory of a naked Garreth Locke rushed into my mind, and I shoved it away.

"Need help?" Ed asked.

"I've got it."

His next words were quiet enough that I wouldn't have heard them if my ears weren't unusually good. "You don't have to do everything yourself, you know."

Yes, I did.

I was the only one I could count on. Life had beaten that lesson into me early enough. I didn't even count on Meg, my only friend, so I certainly wasn't going to be looking to Ed for help. Especially with my precious bike.

I waited until he turned to look down the alley, then gripped the handlebar and lifted the heavy front of the bike a little bit off the ground. It was normally a job for two people or a hydraulic lift, but I was used to doing it on my own. I didn't want Ed seeing that I was freakishly strong, however.

Quickly, I checked the wheel for wobbling and found that the damned thing was loose again. I torqued the axel nut with my free hand, then lowered the bike before Ed turned back around.

The fix worked, and satisfaction surged through me.

Ready to get the hell out of there, I swung my leg over the machine and nodded at Ed. "Have a good night, Ed."

He nodded shortly. Pulling a pack of cigarettes out of his pocket, he turned to look down the alley.

My bike's engine roared as I pulled away from the hotel.

Thank God this hellish day was over.

The sun set as I drove toward the shit part of town. At one point, it felt like I was being followed—that prickle was unmistakable. Unless I was just being paranoid.

Didn't matter. I'd learned long ago not to ignore my hard-won instincts. I might be a maid now, but I hadn't always been one.

Fortunately, I knew the streets of Seattle like the back of my hand, and I lost whoever was following me within ten minutes. By the time I pulled up to my little apartment, I was ready for a dinner of Ramen for one.

Instead, I found a letter.

Immediately, my gaze snagged on the return address. *Seattle School of Business.*

Holy fates, it was here.

But the letter was so thin. Wasn't that bad? Didn't college acceptances usually come in big packets?

My hand shook, and it took me three tries to open the envelope. I fumbled with the paper and finally got it unfolded.

Tears blurred my eyes as I read the first words.

We are pleased to accept you to the Seattle School of Business.

4

Lyra

Morning came too early, and I was only half awake as I rode my bike back toward work. I'd spent a long, lonely night with an old copy of *Pride and Prejudice,* trying to focus on the book instead of the memory of Garreth Locke in the shower.

It hadn't worked. Even worse, he'd followed me into my dreams. The fact that I hadn't kissed a guy—much less gone any further—in over a year was readily apparent by the direction my dreams had taken.

And of course, my imaginary version of Garreth Locke was a genius in the sack. I shook the thought away and turned my bike onto the road that led to the hotel. With any luck, someone would have already made coffee in the break room. It would taste like old motor oil, but it was better than paying for a cup. Maybe I'd get extra lucky and there would be a birthday today.

Free cake.

I loved cake. Free cake, even more. Particularly since that was the only kind I could afford.

As I turned the bike into the alley where I parked, I spotted the sleeping form of the homeless man who often took up residence near the hotel.

I stopped the bike and pulled a dollar from my pocket, tucking it under the battered old coffee mug by his head. He snored away, and I grinned.

He'd never seen me, and that was how I liked it. Ed said he was a grumpy bastard who chose to be homeless, but that was none of my business.

By the time I parked my bike, it was five minutes before my shift started. I grabbed my bag and slung it over my shoulder, then skulked into the back hall of the hotel, praying I could avoid Boris.

I wasn't so lucky.

He waited right by the time punch cards.

"You're late." He glared at me with beady eyes.

My gaze flicked up to the clock over his head. I wasn't late, but I said nothing, just nodded.

He smiled, satisfied. Boris liked to pick on people for the hell of it. Since I didn't care about him, but I *did* care about keeping this job, I let him do it. Hell, how would I

Midnight Moon

stop him, anyway? Punching him in the nose was what I wanted to do, and that sure as hell wasn't an option.

Instead, I clocked in and headed to the changing room.

Unfortunately, there was no birthday cake, but there was an old pot of coffee, and I slugged down a quick cup as I collected my cart.

As I was leaving the staff room, Tina, Kate, and Becca entered, laughing, and chatting about something that had happened at a bar last night.

Envy flared briefly, and I nodded at them in greeting when they looked at me.

Once upon a time, they'd asked me to join them, but I'd said no so many times they'd stopped asking. I didn't even go out with Meg, who was my only friend, so I wasn't going to start going out with them.

Still, it was lonely sometimes.

"Get it together," I muttered as I pushed the cart into the hall. Life was easier alone. Minimal friendships— just Meg—and minimal connection. No family.

Definitely no family.

I was making my way through the bottom floor of the hotel where the conference rooms were located when I spotted Garreth Locke.

I nearly stopped in my tracks, my heart leaping into my throat as I met his gaze. Something flickered in his eyes that made heat flush through me.

He recognized me.

Holy tits, he definitely recognized me. I could see it in his eyes. Hell, he was looking at me like he *knew* me. Like he knew my hopes and fears and darkest desires.

I turned on a dime and headed into an empty conference room. Panting, I leaned against the door and stared at the ceiling.

What the hell was happening to me?

Garreth

It's her.

My breath caught in my throat, and suddenly, I couldn't breathe.

I'd had no idea what she looked like, but I'd know her scent anywhere. She was still ten yards away from me, but I caught the faintest hint of it in the bland hotel hallway.

Lavender, honey, and a fresh breeze.

I resisted drawing it deeply into my lungs, but I couldn't look away as she darted through a nearby doorway. Though she was out of sight, her features were imprinted on my mind. Dark hair, big green eyes, full lips. She was slender but strong, a woman who looked like she could get shit done.

"Garreth. Snap out of it, man."

Midnight Moon 29

I blinked, turning to look at Seth, my friend and beta. As second in command of the pack, he was a powerful wolf. The long scar that cut across his face made it clear that he was a man who had seen some shit. But it was the hardness in his eyes that kept people at bay.

"I'm fine." My voice was unexpectedly rough as it left my throat, and I nearly cringed. I would have if alphas did such things.

As it was, I'd trained myself to show little emotion. Wolves were known for being sensualists. Food, music, dance, sex. We loved it all.

But I was alpha, and as such, I had a responsibility to the pack. A particularly important one given my family's history.

Seth frowned, a knowing glint in his eyes. "You're not all right. What is it?"

My gaze moved toward the space where the woman had been standing, and I immediately cursed myself. It had been an unconscious gesture, but it was enough for Seth to notice.

"The woman." Seth's face cleared as understanding dawned. "Her scent. I thought it was familiar, but I didn't place it at first. She was in your suite yesterday."

I nodded. "She's a housekeeper in the hotel, it seems."

"You didn't see her while she was there?"

"Just missed her." But was that the explanation for

her presence? Something as simple as the fact that she was a housekeeper in the hotel, and she was doing her job?

But no. If she'd just been cleaning, she would have left through the front door.

"She's not the staff member assigned to your suite," Seth said. "You were very specific that it was meant to be the same person."

I nodded. It was a common precaution I took when staying in human hotels. One housekeeper meant less opportunity for them to discover that something was odd about me.

"Perhaps it was a mix-up," Seth said. From the suspicious glint in his gaze, it was clear he didn't believe it. His eyes narrowed on me. "But there's something more here."

I shook my head casually and met his gaze. "Not sure what you're talking about."

But my heart was still racing, pounding against my ribs like a wild animal that wanted to be set free to run. My wolf *did* want to be set free, to run right toward the woman who smelled like home.

"Holy fates." Seth breathed the words, a shocked expression on his face. "She's your mate."

"I've no idea what—"

"Oh, come on. I've never seen you look so shell-shocked in your life. And your heart is going a mile a minute, your pupils dilated."

Midnight Moon

Clever bastard. His attention to details was one of the things that made him an excellent beta, but it wasn't working in my favor now.

"I don't have a mate."

"Of course, you do. Everyone does."

"She's not pack."

"Right." Disappointment and understanding echoed in Seth's words. "She's not even a wolf. Not sure what she is, but it's not a wolf."

"So, you see the problem."

"Just like your father."

"Just like." My gaze was still riveted on the door the woman had disappeared behind.

My father had been alpha before me. After the death of my human mother when I'd been sixteen, he'd fallen for Marguerite, a woman who wasn't pack. Unlike my mother, Marguerite had been his true mate. That didn't mean she'd been good for him, however. She'd destroyed him. Hell, she'd nearly destroyed our pack.

I wouldn't let the same thing happen to me.

"You're not your father, Garreth. And having your mate by your side would be good at the winter gathering. It would make diplomacy easier. And she might hear things we wouldn't since she's not officially part of our pack."

"I can't afford to risk being near her."

Skepticism pulled at the scar that sliced across Seth's face. "You're too hard on yourself."

A bitter laugh escaped me. "Too hard? Never."

Lyra

After too long of a break in the empty conference room, I returned to my duties. Garreth Locke was gone, and the rest of my day was uneventful.

Until I got outside.

Four hulking men stood at the end of the alley, and I immediately knew who they were.

My father's old mob buddies had found me.

Shit. Triple shit.

My throat tightened as panic made breathing difficult.

After so many years of running, my cover was blown. How the hell was today so eventful? Garreth Locke *and* the mob my father had worked for? It was like I'd drawn an unlucky fortune from a cookie.

It made one thing clear, though—I *had* been followed last night.

One look at them, and I was moving faster than I ever had in my life.

Fortunately, my bike started on the first try. I spun around in a quick U-turn and headed down to the other

Midnight Moon

end of the alley. As I entered onto the street, a car pulled out of its parking spot on the side of the road.

Fear iced my spine.

They'd been waiting for me.

My mother had warned me how persistent and clever they were. Before he'd died, my father had sold me and my mother out to his cronies in crime, promising them we could repay his debt.

Of course, we couldn't.

My mother and I had run, but the stress of it had driven her to drugs, which had killed her when I was fourteen.

Since then, I'd been alone. Ten years, alone.

I'd run and run and run, trying to stay one step ahead of the mob who wanted me to settle my father's debt.

Time's up.

The car behind me revved its engine, speeding up until I could see the men in the front seat when I glanced into my tiny rearview mirrors.

Fear spiked my heartbeat, followed by cold calm.

I'm getting out of this.

I sped up, taking a turn so fast that I had to lean with the bike to keep from overturning. The car was unable to follow, but they'd catch me at the next block.

I drove faster, almost hoping that a cop would catch me going over the limit. Instead, the white car joined me two streets over, speeding alongside my bike as I raced in front of the shops that dotted the street.

The car kept up.

Shit, this wasn't working.

Abruptly, I put on my brakes. The larger car couldn't manage the same. Making a quick U-turn, I flew back down the road.

Adrenaline coursed through my veins as I weaved in and out of traffic, ignoring the outraged drivers honking their horns as they swerved to miss me. I spotted an opening between two cars and took a sharp left turn. My knowledge of Seattle's streets came in handy as I raced home.

Well, that made one thing clear—they'd definitely been following me last night, and I'd lost them before I'd gotten to my apartment. I'd felt it in my bones when I was no longer being followed, and I'd assumed they didn't know where I lived when they hadn't shown up on my doorstep.

I hoped.

With any luck, I'd have enough time to get home and pack a few things before hitting the road.

The idea of running again turned my stomach. I had a *life* here. It kind of sucked, but it was mine. And I had just been accepted to school. My life was about to turn around.

So of course, my miserable father was about to make an appearance, even though he was long dead.

Nope.

I wasn't going to think about him. I was just going to keep moving forward. I'd get myself out of this jam just as I'd gotten myself out of plenty of others.

Finally, I reached my apartment complex. The streets were quiet as I pulled into the parking lot and killed the engine. I took the stairs two at a time up to the third floor, then slammed into my apartment and began grabbing up items I didn't want to leave behind, along with my tiny savings.

My crappy duffel bag was bursting at the seams by the time I headed back through the living room and opened the front door.

Four hulking figures were standing in the hall, and my stomach dropped.

Shit. They *had* known where I lived.

Did I try to fake it?

My gaze raced over them. They were all equally brutal looking, with stupidly huge muscles and square jaws.

Where the hell did the mob find these clowns? They'd be comedic except for the fact that any one of them could snap my spine with his bare hands.

"We've been looking for you." The leader stepped forward, entering my living room with a deadly grace that was petrifying. His silent approach made him even more dangerous and terrifying. With stealth like that, he could sneak into my bedroom while I was asleep and suffocate me.

His eyes were so cold they looked dead.

"I have no idea who you are," I said, my voice shaking.

"There's no point in pretending, Lilibet."

The mention of my real name made my heart jackhammer. "It's Lyra. You've got the wrong girl." I backed toward the bedroom, hoping if I were quick enough, I could make it out the window.

As if.

"We don't have the wrong girl." He cracked his knuckles, and ice shot down my spine. "We've been watching you for quite a while, in fact."

Sickly dread rose in my stomach. Was that true?

"Seriously, you've got—"

"Shut up." His quiet, menacing words had me snapping my mouth shut.

Shit.

I swallowed hard, glancing behind me toward the bedroom.

"Don't bother." His tone was dismissive. "We've got guys in the alley below."

Damn. I drew in a deep breath. It was time to cut the crap. They clearly knew who I was. "What the hell do you want?"

"Your father owed us a lot of money before he died."

Did I try to keep pretending?

Midnight Moon

No, he clearly knew who I was. "That was over ten years ago. And it's not my debt."

"Like I said, it was a *lot* of money. You know how these things work."

I gestured around the crappy apartment full of secondhand furniture. "As if I can afford to pay you back. Look at this place."

"That's why we haven't contacted you until now. You never had anything that could cover your father's debt."

"Well, I haven't won the lottery lately, so you're still shit out of luck."

"I wouldn't say that." He strolled around the living room as if he owned it, his steps slow and deliberate. "Your current job has finally proved interesting."

"Finally?"

"We've watched you over the years. Kept track. First, you lived at Remy Street and were engaged in a bit of petty crime. Next, you moved to an apartment on Kingston Avenue and upped your skills. Jewelry stores, wasn't it?"

"Only the big chains that could afford to lose a few little pieces." My stomach turned sour. Kingston had been *years* ago. I'd been a teenager. And yet they'd known where I was?

The knowledge that they'd been stalking me all this time chilled me to the marrow of my bones.

"You have a friend at the hotel, don't you? Megan Marrow?"

"Are you threatening Meg?" Acid twisted my stomach.

"I see you're starting to understand. If you don't do this, she's dead." The cold determination in his voice made my soul freeze. "Do I need to continue?"

"No." I believed him, wholeheartedly. They'd always known where I was. There was no way to keep hiding—not if they had this kind of reach. And it didn't matter anyway because they were threatening Meg. "What do you want?"

"We want you to do a little job for us, that's all."

A little job.

Famous words when they came from the mob.

5

Lyra

"You want me to *what?*" They had to be kidding.

"You're not deaf, and you're not stupid. You know what we asked you. Steal the book from Garreth Locke, and your debt is paid in full. You won't owe us a cent."

"No way I'm doing that." My mind raced. Garreth led their rival criminal organization, so they basically wanted me to be the filling in a mob sandwich. No way in hell. "And how do you even know he has it?"

"Oh, we have our ways."

"That's super vague."

"You think I'd reveal our sources to you?" The derision in his tone suggested that it had taken him a lot of effort to find out how Garreth had the book, and I wasn't going to be the recipient of that information.

"Fine. But I was just accepted into business school. Let me go and I'll repay you with honest work."

The bastard just laughed. *Laughed.*

"I don't think so," he said. "You'll do as you're told. Then maybe, if you're lucky, your slate will be wiped clean."

"It's not even *my* slate." I hadn't seen my father for months before he died, and that had been a decade ago. "This is insane."

"It's life, honey."

"Bastards."

He just grinned. "Now you're getting the picture. So, what do you say? Are you going to do it, or is your friend going to die?"

I looked at the four of them, then at the shitty bag I'd packed to resume my life on the run.

Looks like that's not happening.

Not if they were threatening to kill Meg.

"Fine." Saying it made my stomach turn. "I'll do it. What's so valuable about this book anyway?"

"Let's just say it's very rare."

"So, it's worth a ton of money."

"Essentially." He shrugged, as if it weren't interesting at all.

"Fine. But when it's done, we're through. You and

your cronies forget you ever knew my family. And you leave my friend alone."

"You've got a deal."

It wasn't the patronizing tone that caught my attention the most—it was the look in his eyes. Like he was lying. "I need some assurance that you're really going to let me go after this."

The right side of his face twitched, a tic that was almost unnoticeable but revealed his irritation. And his lies.

"Yeah, that's what I thought," I said. "How do I know that—"

He took a step, reaching me in half second. Before I knew what was happening, he had his hand around my neck and my back pressed to the wall. Pressure crushed my windpipe until I could no longer breathe. My lungs burned and stars burst behind my eyelids.

Fear chilled me to the bone.

He would kill me.

Whatever power I'd thought I had here disappeared like the figment it had been. As consciousness faded, I opened my eyes. My attacker's ugly face swam in front of me, a satisfied smirk stretching his lips into an ugly smile.

"I see you understand your predicament," he said.

I nodded as best I could with his hand around my throat.

He released me, and I slumped against the wall,

gasping raggedly through my bruised throat. As oxygen returned to my body, anger followed it. I looked up at the men who'd invaded my tiny apartment. In their nice clothes and expensive shoes, they made it seem more ramshackle and miserable than ever.

But it was mine.

This was *my* life. And Meg was *my* friend. My only friend.

If saving her meant doing this job, then I'd do it. And I'd find a way to get out from under their thumb forever, no matter how long it took.

"We'll expect you to have the book to us within three days," he said. "Don't forget what happens if you fail. Oh, and don't think you can tell Garreth Locke what's going on. He won't protect you, and we'll *definitely* kill your friend if you try to rat us out. Same goes if you try to tip her off. We've got someone on her at all times, and if she changes her routine or tries to run for it, we'll nab her."

"You've covered all the bases, haven't you?" Bitterness edged my voice.

"Oh, most definitely." He pulled a phone from his pocket and pressed a few buttons, then turned it to face me. It was a live video feed of the outside of her apartment, clearly filmed by someone who was stalking her.

The sight solidified my determination. "I can do it."

I watched them leave, my heart thundering. I wanted to call Meg, but I couldn't, could I?

Garreth

I stepped out of my car, inhaling deeply of the fresh sea air that blew off Puget Sound. It rustled the tall pines behind me. My breath fogged in front of my face, condensing on the chill air.

I should be in Seattle still, but after seeing my mate, I'd needed to return home briefly.

Home.

Olympia always smelled like this, and it was the best scent in the world.

Until I'd smelled my mate.

No. I turned my mind from the thought and looked toward the moon. It hung heavy in the sky, still not full. We weren't the sort of werewolves compelled to turn on the night of the full moon, though we did prefer to run beneath it.

Sensing the direction of my thoughts, my wolf went wild inside me. The beast was desperate to come out. To run.

I was desperate to let him, especially now that I was on the massive estate that my pack called home. Feeling the wind in my fur and the ground beneath my feet made me feel alive. Too alive, sometimes. I was afraid of turning into my father, a man who'd given in to his baser instincts at the expense of the pack.

I'd never be him.

"Later," I murmured. I could just as easily do it now —shift and race through the beautiful winter night— but denying myself only honed my control.

After the way I'd behaved when I'd seen my mate, I needed all the honing I could get.

I drew in a ragged breath and strode down to the water. For the most part, our pack lived in the massive house that sat on the rocky cliff at the edge of the sound. The building was the size of a damned castle, but very modern, with sleek lines and huge panes of glass that provided a phenomenal view.

Golden light glowed from the windows, welcoming any wolves who would arrive later at night.

I ignored the house, however, and made my way toward the long, wooden pier that jutted out into the sound. Our access to the water was one of the reasons our land was so highly prized. That, and the fact that we owned thousands of acres of woodland that had been bespelled to be repellent to humans. As humans had multiplied across the west coast, land like ours had become insanely valuable to members of the magical community. It was one of the few places of its kind on the entire continent.

The wind picked up as I stepped onto the dock, cutting into the suit I wore. I despised the things, but

Midnight Moon

they were necessary for my visits to Seattle. It helped me blend with the humans. To them, I looked like just another boring businessman.

When I was home, I preferred plaid flannel and denim. But I was only home for a short visit, so there was no point in changing.

As I strode across the dock, I passed several power-boats and a few small sailing skiffs that the pups used. I kept my gaze glued to the large wooden sailboat at the end of the pier. It bobbed on the small waves, the metal rigging clanging against the mast. The small windows shone with warm light, but the owner wasn't inside the cabin.

She was sitting at the bow, staring out over the water toward the darkness in the distance. Her long red hair tumbled down her back, and when the wind changed direction, I could smell her magic. Lemon and grass. Not a shifter's scent, but she wasn't a shifter.

Kate was a witch, one of the few in the US without a coven, and she made her home part time with my pack. We gave her a place to dock her boat, along with protection. In exchange, she occasionally helped us with her magic.

"Garreth." She didn't turn around as she said my name, her long hair blowing in the wind.

"How did you know it was me?" I stopped on the dock beside her. "Witches have a terrible sense of smell."

She laughed. "I have my ways."

"I'm hoping you can use those ways to help me out."

"Oh?" She looked at me, then, eyebrows raised. Kate was beautiful in a delicate way, and there might have been something between us when she'd first arrived if I hadn't been so determined to avoid any attachment and she hadn't been so heartbroken—by what, I'd never known.

"What do you want?" she asked.

"I need help with my mate." Even the words sounded foreign on my tongue.

Her eyebrows shot even higher, surprise sparkling in her eyes. "Your mate, you say?"

I nodded. "I saw her in the city."

"Congratulations."

I felt a scowl cut across my face, an unconscious display of emotion that annoyed me. "Not in order."

"Why not? Every wolf is always thrilled to find their mate."

She was right. It was usually a cause for celebration. It wasn't a love at first sight thing with most fated mates, but it was fate's way of saying *this person is perfect for you.*

If neither party totally screwed it up, it was often the best thing that ever happened to them.

"It's not an option for me," I said. "I need a way to break the bond."

She held up her hand. "Wait a minute. I'm going to need to know why it's not an option. Because if I've ever

Midnight Moon

seen someone who could use a little comfort in their life, it's you."

"I'm fine." I crossed my arms and glared. "There's nothing wrong with my life."

"Sure. All those nights working alone must be such a blast."

"You know the pack needs me."

She waved a hand dismissively, and I was equal parts annoyed and gratified. Even though she occasionally lived on our land, Kate wasn't pack. Having a person who didn't rely on me had turned out to be very valuable. She gave good advice, and I never needed to worry that she wanted something I couldn't give.

"Sure, they need you," she said. "But you know what they say on airplanes. Put the oxygen mask on yourself first."

"I'm breathing just fine, thanks."

"You know what I mean. You're going to wither up and die if you stay alone all the time. I've never even seen you date."

"Doesn't mean I don't." But I didn't. She didn't need to know that, though. "So, will you help me or not?"

"Of course, I will. But first, I want to know why it's so damned important to get her out of your life. Because that's just plain crazy, and I'm not going to do it unless you tell me why."

I pinched the bridge of my nose and stared down at the wide wooden slats of the dock. I could just barely make out the dark water below. "You weren't here when my father was alpha."

"No. I've heard stories, though. No leadership. Young wolves leaving for other packs, like the one in the city."

Just the mention of the City Pack raised my hackles. They were the entire reason my pack was falling apart. "You heard right. But his mate was the reason for that."

"What?" She frowned.

"She wasn't pack. Which is highly unusual for us, but she was his mate, so no one said anything. It was years before we realized that she owed her loyalty to the City Pack." The shifters living in Seattle were a mixed group—mostly mountain lions, but a few bears, and now two dozen of our wolves—and she'd been one of the mountain lions.

"Holy fates." She breathed out a shocked sound. "So, when the pack was falling apart and you guys were losing members to the City Pack, it was partially because of her?"

I nodded. "She was polluting his mind. The City Pack hoped that if they could get enough of our pack into theirs, they could eventually take over our land. We've lost two dozen of our youngest wolves to their poaching."

I occasionally saw them in the city when I visited, but they crossed the street to avoid me.

"Bastards." Her face suddenly turned sad. "Is that why your father killed himself?"

I nodded, my chest tightening. "He realized one day what was going on. It was like he woke up out of a fog, and the truth of his mate crushed him. But discovering how far the pack had fallen was what ended him. He knew he needed to pass it on."

How he'd done it had been horrifying.

I still remembered coming home from the army and finding his body hanging from the rafters of his quarters. The sight had hit me in the gut and haunted me to this day, along with the contents of the letter he'd left me.

After pulling his body down, I'd found it in his pocket with my name on it. I'd known he was becoming increasingly distracted, but I'd had no idea that such a sickness had overcome him.

The contents of the letter were still emblazoned on my mind. He'd begged me not to make his mistake—not to fall for my mate the way he had and lose his way. Then he'd begged me to fix it. To bring the younger wolves back into the fold.

After my father's terrible last years as alpha, the City Pack was now stronger than ours. We were at risk of losing everything.

I couldn't be distracted by a woman. Especially not my mate.

"So, you've been roped in to solving the pack's problems." Though the sadness on her face had faded, I could still hear it in her voice.

"I'm fine, Kate. I trained my whole life for this. I want to be alpha." I'd hoped I'd have more time in the human military—I enjoyed the time away from pack politics and my enlistment was a way to honor my human mother—but I'd always known I'd come home to serve as alpha of the Olympia Pack.

"And you're a good one. But I don't think you really need to give up your shot at love."

"I can't risk it—not after what happened to my father." I'd die before I let the pack down. Before I broke my promise to my father's memory. "Will you help me?"

"What exactly do you want to do to her?"

"I want her to forget that I exist."

"So, she knows you're her mate?"

"I think not, since she isn't a wolf. She doesn't have our sense of smell. But she is interested in me for some reason."

"Not a wolf?" Surprise sounded in her voice.

"Another reason I can't be with her. My father's mate was a mountain lion and look where it got us. I don't know what kind of magic she has, but I can't afford to trust her."

"You need to start trusting those outside the pack," she said. "You've been too reclusive."

"I'm not here for therapy. Will you help me, or will you leave?"

Her jaw dropped slightly. "Are you threatening to evict me?"

I raked a hand through my hair, frustration clawing at me. "No. That was wrong of me."

"Damn straight. This is a mutually beneficial arrangement, you know." She gestured between the boat and the dock. "My magic is valuable. And yes, I'll help you, even though I don't agree with what you're doing. Just the forgetfulness spell?"

"I'd also like to know why she broke into my hotel room."

"Oh, the plot thickens!"

"Don't sound so excited."

She shrugged. "What? It's a bit dull out here at night."

"You could always—"

She raised a hand, cutting me off before I could finish the offer to let her stay in the big house with the rest of the pack. "No. You know I don't want to."

"Just don't know why." Every time I offered, she turned it down. I could almost feel the loneliness in her, but she stayed on her boat. There'd been hurt in her eyes when she'd first arrived, but she'd never shared why.

"Don't worry about it. Let's talk about what you need. Why can't you just ask her?"

"Do you think she'll tell me the truth?"

She frowned. "No, I suppose not."

"Exactly."

She tapped her chin thoughtfully. "I can whip up a

truth potion so you can figure out what she's after, but that will take a few days."

"Do it, please."

"All right. In the meantime, I can give you a selective memory erasing spell. It's tricky to use, though. You'll have to get her to lower the guard on her mind so you can use it."

"How do I get her to do that?"

"A few ways. Make her fall in love with you is the best, but in a pinch, you can get her to tell you a valuable secret. While she's confiding in you, her guard should be down. Then you deploy the spell. It'll sneak inside her subconscious and delete any memory of you."

"She won't feel that she's my mate?"

"She shouldn't."

"Good. Except... It's going to be damned hard to get her to lower her guard."

"*You* could always forget *her*."

"No." The word came out too sharply, and I wanted to turn away. I resisted, which allowed me to see the smug look on Kate's face.

"I knew you liked her," she said.

"I don't even know her." But I didn't want to forget her. If all I could have of her was a tiny memory, I wanted it. And anyway, it would be unwise to forget her. If I ran into her again, my wolf would probably still recognize her. Nothing would keep him from that. "Do you have the forgetfulness spell now?"

Midnight Moon

"I do." She climbed to her feet. "Just wait a moment."

I focused on the silence all around as she climbed down into the cabin of the large wooden sailboat. Through the tiny windows, I saw her searching for something.

She returned with a small bag in her hand and gave it to me. "Get her to lower her guard. When that happens, press the small charm to her skin and say the word *finite*."

She pronounced it with a flare at the end.

"She'll think I'm insane."

"You'll be scrambling her brains, so she won't remember it."

Guilt struck. "She'll be all right though, won't she?"

"Of course." Insult sounded in Kate's voice. "I'm excellent at my job."

"Right, my apologies." I raised my hands in a placating gesture. "You're the best."

"Damn straight. But good luck. I think you're going to need it."

"I'm sure I will." I thanked her and made my way toward the woods at the back of the property.

I knew I should get back to Seattle ASAP to continue preparing for the winter gathering, but I wanted to run. Needed to.

As I stepped through the tree line, I called upon my wolf, feeling the magic bubble in my veins. It roared through me, taking over my body and transforming me into a massive black wolf.

As I ran through the forest with the wind in my fur, everything felt better. Clearer.

Protect.

My pack needed me, and that was all there was to it.

6

Lyra

The next day, I began to prepare for the theft of a lifetime. Just the idea of trying it scared the crap out of me.

As I walked into the staff room at the start of my shift, it felt like everyone was looking at me. As if they knew what I was going to do.

I shook the thought away and punched my timecard, then changed quickly, grateful that Boris wasn't around. I needed to find out how long Garreth Locke would be here, and I certainly couldn't ask around. It would be far too suspicious when the theft was discovered. I didn't want anyone to think I was interested in him.

The only way for me to find out when he was leaving was to check one of the computers in the office. They contained the same records as the computers at reception, and I could see how long the penthouse would be occupied.

My chance came shortly after my lunch break. Most people were out at the nearby Mexican place, but as usual, I'd stayed back to eat alone.

Not that I had any kind of appetite.

Instead, I'd been biding my time. The back office was empty when I slipped through the quiet hall and hurried toward it. My heart thundered as I pulled up the schedule, frantically scanning for the info I needed so that I could get the hell out of there.

I hated this kind of subterfuge. Give me a building to climb any day.

"What are you doing?" Meg's voice cut through my absorption in the hotel records, and I jumped.

"Shit." I tried to wipe the guilt from my face. "You scared me. I was just checking to see how slammed we are this week."

Technically, I wasn't supposed to do that, and I never did. But it was something that I'd seen other housekeepers do. We could get out early if our workload was particularly light.

"Oh?" Interest sparked in Meg's voice. "Hoping to get off early this week? Got a date or something?"

"Yeah. A date with Ben & Jerry's." I desperately wanted to tell her what was going on and that she needed to run for her life, but the mobster's threat lingered in my mind.

I couldn't risk it.

"Ha! That can't be it."

Shit. I had to tell her something. "I got accepted to the Seattle School of Business. I was hoping to get off early enough to celebrate on Friday."

Her eyes widened. "That's amazing! I know how badly you wanted that. I'm coming with you to celebrate!"

"Yeah." Guilt tugged at me, but I was distracted by the sound of voices coming from the hall. I clicked out of the computer and stood. "Better go before we're caught."

She nodded and spun around. I followed her from the room, my heart pounding.

"I like the scarf." She pointed to the small fake silk scarf I'd tied around the bruises on my throat. "Boris will have a shit fit if he sees it, though."

I touched the fabric, swallowing hard despite the pain in my throat. "Then I'll just be sure not to run into him."

"Ha, he's everywhere."

She was right, and I hated that about working there. Boris was like a giant spider that lurked in every corner, his many eyes watching as you tried to keep your head above water.

We passed the other three housekeepers and I nodded, but my mind was on Meg.

"What are you up to this week?" I asked. "Any date night plans with Tommy?"

I didn't actually care about Tommy—he wasn't good enough for her, as far as I was concerned—but it would be safer for her to be with him while the mob was watching her.

I also wanted to know when she'd have an alibi. When Garreth Locke realized he'd been robbed, the first person they would suspect would be Meg.

She had access to his room after all, and a good reason to be there. I couldn't let her take the fall for me. She'd be protected by the fact that they wouldn't see her going into the suite in the evening, but that might not be enough. She needed an airtight alibi before I made my move.

"Yeah!" Excitement sparked in her voice. "We're going to a party tonight. Big one. Want to come?"

"Um, maybe we can hang out later this week?"

"Sure. I'm free every other night. Just me and the cat hanging out."

Damn it. The cat was a shit alibi. If tonight was the only night she was covered, I was going to have to make my move. And frankly, I needed to get the mob off her back fast.

"I'm off to finish my shift," Meg said. "See you later this week."

Midnight Moon

"Awesome."

She grinned. "If you change your mind about the party tonight, let me know."

"Yeah. I will." Maybe it could be my alibi too, though I wasn't planning to be a suspect. There was no reason for me to be in the room after all. "And Meg? Hang out with Tommy a lot. I think you guys are great for each other."

I'd pay for that lie later, but it was worth it.

"You like him?" Her face lit up. "Awesome."

"Yeah. Just, you know, be careful. It's dangerous out there."

"Um, all right." She clearly thought I was being a bit weird but didn't press me on it. "You, too."

The rest of my shift went far too quickly. No matter how hard I tried, it was impossible to get my mind off what I'd attempt tonight. Frankly, I couldn't believe I was going to do it.

You have to.

The memory of the mob boss's hand around my neck made me reach up and fiddle with the scarf covering the bruises. It'd be impossible to avoid questions if anyone saw them, and I couldn't bear to look at them in the mirror.

By the time my shift was over, I was nearly vibrating with anxiety. I had a plan and the skills, but I felt guilty as hell.

But what's a book compared to my life? Garreth Locke might not even notice it was missing.

With any luck, he wouldn't go out this evening and I wouldn't be able to attempt the theft.

Nope. That was stupid.

Failure was not an option.

Which was why I found myself waiting at the bus stop across from the hotel later that night. I was mostly hidden inside the bus shelter, but I had a great vantage point of the front of the building. If Garreth Locke left for the evening, I'd see him.

I fiddled with the scarf around my neck as I waited, using the memory of the threat to Meg to fuel my determination.

Finally, I spotted him by the valet stand. He had two companions—a man and a woman. They were the same ones who often accompanied him, and I briefly envied him the ease of friendship they apparently had.

I held my breath as the valet brought their car around. It was a top-of-the-line Land Rover, of course. Only the best for Garreth Locke. When they pulled out into traffic, I stood. Every move I made felt like an out-of-body experience, but I kept myself moving forward.

No one noticed me as I headed toward the alley to the fire escape. I'd debated my approach, deciding that the most dangerous one was also the best. The interior of the hotel was covered with security cameras. The exterior, not so much.

Midnight Moon 61

Even better, the cops would probably never expect a thief to have come from the outside. The building was just too difficult to climb. For a normal person, at least. I had no idea why I had my weird skill, but I was grateful for it.

The alley was silent as I entered it, and I wasted no time ascending the old fire escape to the top floor. I still had to climb along the outside of the building and turn the corner so that I could get to the window I'd escaped from before.

I prayed it was still unlocked.

Finally, I reached the top of the fire escape. It was silent, besides the wind that whipped my hair back from my face. In the distance, I could see the dark surface of Puget Sound reflecting the city lights.

Anxiety tightened my chest. Until I'd stood there, I hadn't really believed I was going to do it.

But I was.

It was go-time.

I drew a deep breath and climbed onto the side of the building. I was still dressed in my maid's uniform. If I got caught inside the room, I would say I was delivering more soaps. I'd thrown a black coat over it to conceal me while I climbed the building. Fortunately, this part of town was quiet in the evening. The cool wind off the water kept the walkers away, and there were no restaurants to attract a late-night crowd.

Carefully, I made my way along the side of the building, moving more quickly in front of the windows in case a guest was inside the room. My heart thundered loudly in my ears, the threat of getting caught keeping me on my toes.

When I finally reached the window to Garreth Locke's suite, relief rushed through me. It was difficult to pry the window open from the outside, and there was a terrifying moment where it stuck.

"No, no, no," I muttered, trying to jimmy the window open.

Finally, it opened with a whoosh and slid upward. I scrambled inside, my heart racing as I found my footing on the carpet. I loved climbing buildings, but I appreciated solid ground just as much.

"In and out, in and out," I muttered. My gaze went immediately to the bedside table.

The book was gone.

Cold sweat formed on my skin.

This couldn't be happening.

In my head, I'd dart in, grab the book, then dart back out. But it was gone.

Shit, shit, shit.

Quickly, I moved to Plan B. I shut the window, then stripped off my dark jacket and laid it behind the table near the window, concealing it. My pockets were full of tiny soaps—my weak cover for being inside the suite—but I hoped I wouldn't have to use them.

Midnight Moon 63

My heart thundered as I began to search the suite for the book. Where the hell was it?

Not in the closet, where I found a row of the impeccably tailored suits that Garreth Locke wore religiously. It wasn't in the bathroom, either, which smelled like him. The scent was intoxicating, tempting me to stay and breathe it in until I got high.

No time for that.

I moved to the living room, frantically searched every surface and under every cushion.

Still, no book.

When I heard the faint sound of footsteps, it took me a moment to process it.

He's coming.

Crap, crap, crap. He must have forgotten something in the suite.

I sprinted for the bathroom, tucking myself behind the door just as I heard him enter the suite. I held my breath, wondering if I was going to have to deploy my weak cover.

He moved so silently I didn't hear him. One moment, I was cowering against the wall, and the next, a big hand had me by the arm and was pulling me out of the bathroom and into the bedroom. He pushed me up against the wall, towering over me.

Shock rooted me to the spot as I stared up at him. He filled my vision, his sharp cheekbones and square jaw barely softened by the full lips that pulled into a frown.

The long, glorious black hair was pulled into a low ponytail at the nape of his neck. Heat burned in his golden eyes, and he was so beautiful that it made my breath catch. Scary as hell, too.

My arm burned where he gripped me. His touch was gentle, but it felt like it would leave a brand.

Time stopped as I stared at him. His pupils dilated and his full lips parted as his gaze raced over my face. The intensity of it was unlike anything I'd ever experienced. He inhaled deeply, seeming unable to help himself.

As his eyelids went to half mast, I couldn't help but get the impression that he liked how I smelled. *A lot.*

I drew in a ragged breath, his forest scent wrapping around me and making my head spin.

I liked how he smelled, too. Loved it. All I could think about was burying my face in his neck to inhale more of it, then moving my lips along his smooth skin, kissing every inch of him I could reach.

What the hell was happening to me?

The tension that tightened the air between us was like nothing I'd ever felt before. More visions of him kissing me flashed in my mind, and a desperate desire unfurled within me.

I want you.

I'd never felt so strongly about anyone in my entire life. But suddenly, all I could think of was leaning up to kiss him.

Midnight Moon

Miraculously, he seemed to be thinking the same thing. The heat in his eyes burned me to my core, and as he leaned down, my breath caught in my throat.

This is it.

He's going to kiss me.

Anticipation raced through me. My mind went blank, leaving me a vibrating bundle of need. It was insane how fast and hard the desire hit me.

Just before his lips touched mine, he shook his head as if coming out of a trance.

The heat in his gaze was replaced by ice, and he stepped back, releasing his hold on me.

"What are you doing here?" His voice was cold, and I felt like I'd been splashed with a bucket of freezing seawater.

I gasped, swallowing hard and blinking up at him.

Shit, what was my cover story again? My head was still spinning from the unnaturally strong attraction that had made me lose my wits.

Finally, it came to me.

"Just dropping off some more toiletries." My voice shook as I reached into my pocket and withdrew the tiny bottles, feeling like an idiot.

Suddenly, my plan didn't feel so clever. How had I not realized it was super dumb?

That's because you didn't expect to have to use it.

His eyes narrowed on my hand.

"I'll just be going then." I stepped to the side, planning to veer around him and escape through the door. "Have a good night."

He stepped in front of me so quickly that I nearly slammed into him. He caught my arms, stopping me an inch before we collided. Indecision flickered in his gaze, as if he were considering yanking me against him again.

Do it.

"I really need to get going." I pulled back from him, and he frowned as if he didn't want to let me go. When his hands lost contact with my upper arms, I should have felt freed.

I didn't.

He seemed to recover from his surprise quickly. "What are you really doing here?"

"Refilling your toiletries. I work with housekeeping." I gestured to my uniform, remembering the jacket I'd hidden behind his table. *Please don't find it.*

At least I'd closed the window behind me.

"You're not assigned to this room. It's always the same person, and that's not you."

"She asked me to step in." Panic made me say the words, but guilt followed on its heels. I shouldn't be throwing Meg under the bus. "I mean, I saw that she needed help and—"

"Just tell me why you're really here."

Well shit.

Garreth Locke was not a man who would buy my bullshit.

7

Garreth

She was lying, and she was terrible at it.

It took everything I had to keep my focus on what was important, instead of my insanely strong desire to yank her into my arms and kiss her until I lost my mind.

I'd never felt anything like the mate bond. The attraction was nearly impossible to resist. It felt like we were wrapped up in our own world of desire.

Focus.

What was she here for? I'd asked around about her. She'd worked at the hotel for years, even before I'd become a regular guest.

Which meant that being in this hotel wasn't about

me. It was just coincidence, unless a seer had told her that this was where she'd meet me one day.

Did she know she was my mate?

From the confusion and fear in her golden eyes, my guess was she didn't. The memory of her arms beneath my hands made my heart race and my palms itch to touch her again. For the brief moment when I'd nearly kissed her, it was heaven.

It was dangerous to want her, but I did. Desperately. Being close to her made my wolf go mad, as if he wanted to burst through my skin and nuzzle her face with his own.

I couldn't blame him, even though I knew better.

Because she was up to something big, and I wanted to figure out what it was. The sentry posted on the street told me she'd climbed the side of the building again. No human could do that, nor many supernaturals.

"Cut the games," I said, and she flinched almost imperceptibly.

Guilt shot through me. I didn't want to frighten her, even though scaring her away was probably the smartest thing I could do.

But no—if I wanted to know what she was up to, a more subtle approach was required. There were still a few days until Kate finished making the truth serum that I would use to find out why she was stalking me. Maybe I could use this time to my advantage.

Midnight Moon

A plan began to form, inspired by Seth's words from earlier today. "You work at the hotel?"

"I do." She gave a tight smile. "Housekeeping."

"Hmm. Perhaps you could help me with something." I couldn't believe I hadn't thought of this before.

She shot me a horrified look. "Ew. No."

My brows shot up. "What?"

"Oh." Her mouth rounded in surprise. "You didn't mean anything sleazy, did you?"

"No. Do you get that often?"

She shrugged. "From the dudes on business trips."

"Bastards." But hang on... "You almost just kissed me, and now you're saying *ew*?"

"I was caught up in the moment. And I wouldn't kiss you if I thought you were a sleaze."

"Fair enough. But it's not what I meant. I could use your help at a meeting this weekend. I'd like you to pose as my...partner."

"Partner?"

I didn't want to say mate in case she didn't know what she was to me, and that was the first title that had popped to mind.

"Girlfriend," I clarified, though I disliked the weak human term. But Seth had a point. She could be useful at the gathering. And until I knew what she was up to, I didn't want her out of my sight.

Her brows shot halfway to her hairline. "Come again, now?"

"I'd like you to attend the winter gathering with me." Every supernatural on the west coast knew about it, whether they were a shifter or not, so she'd already be aware of it. Once a year, the leaders of the various packs met at a remote ski lodge in the mountainous part of Washington to hash out differences and restore bonds.

This year, I was going to attempt diplomacy with the City Pack and address our problem. They had no land of their own and were trying to steal ours. Their constant incursions onto our turf were becoming more common. If they hadn't poached so many of our youth, I'd attack them with brute force. It was my preferred method for driving away enemies.

However, twenty percent of their pack was made up of former members of mine. They had family back at Olympia. It was my job to reunite those families.

As much as I hated the idea of it, I had to try one last stab at a compromise before this ended with bloodshed.

The City Pack had agreed to negotiate. They had stronger numbers, but we had the best turf. Surely there was something we could work out.

Except, I didn't know if I could trust them. Not after what had happened with my father.

"I'm going to need more info," she said.

"My rivals, the City Pack, will be there, and I want to know if they are dealing honestly with me. I'd like you to come as my date. If they try to get information out of you about me, report back."

Midnight Moon 71

"So, you want me to go to this meeting and be a litmus test for whether they're being honest with you?"

"Exactly." They'd used my father's mate against him. Perhaps they would do the same with mine. I'd dangle her in front of them like bait and see if they took it. She'd be safe with me at her side, and I could find out how trustworthy they were.

Hell, maybe she was already working for them, considering she'd snuck into my room. If that was the case, I wanted to find out. I'd keep her close until Kate finished the truth serum. Meantime, I'd try to get her to lower her guard so I could use the spell that would make her forget me.

"I don't know." She backed away from me slowly. "I'm not really used to doing this kind of thing."

"You don't need any special practice."

She frowned.

"I also won't tell your boss I found you in here." The fact that she'd been working here so long made me think she might not be a member of the City Pack, but I still couldn't trust her. She *had* climbed the side of a building to get to my suite. I needed to keep her close until I could figure out why.

Anger flushed her cheeks. "Are you blackmailing me into helping you?"

"Yes. If you don't, you'll lose your job."

"Bastard."

"I'm glad you've agreed to come."

"I haven't. Not yet." Her brow furrowed as she thought. "I really can't afford to lose my job. I've got the weekend off, but if this takes longer than expected, Boris will sack me. So, I'm going to need payment too. Twenty thousand."

It was steep, but worth it. "Agreed. You're no longer being blackmailed. We're now business partners."

"The hell we are. Unless you back off on the threat to tell my boss, you are *definitely* still blackmailing me."

"I'm not backing off of that one."

"So, it's blackmail with payment, because I want it clear I wouldn't be doing this otherwise."

"That's fine. Glad to see you're willing to help. Can you ski?"

Lyra

"What the hell?" I stared at Garreth Locke, stunned. "You want me to ski? Like, with two poles and snow?"

"The gathering is at a ski lodge in the central part of the state."

Holy shit, this was getting out of control. What the hell was he up to, trying to get me to pretend I was his girlfriend at a meeting? It was like the plot of *Pretty*

Midnight Moon   73

Woman with theft, rather than prostitution--or so I hoped.

And he was acting like I should know what the winter gathering and City Pack were. It had to be a company of some kind, and this had to be a corporate retreat. I could probably find more info on the internet.

But this was exactly the opportunity I needed to find the book. I'd only demanded money because I hadn't wanted to seem too eager to go along. The last thing I needed was for him to suspect me. Normally, the idea of twenty thousand dollars would excite me. But with Meg's life on the line, I couldn't even think about it.

"Yeah, I can ski." I'd never done it before, but I was athletic. How hard could it be? "And I'll snoop around at this meeting and see if anyone tries to recruit me." Should be easy enough.

He smiled, though it didn't fully reach his eyes. The only time I'd seen him with his guard down had been when he'd first spotted me in the suite. For the briefest moment, it had felt like he knew me. After that, a shield had gone up over his face.

"Good. We leave tomorrow morning. In the meantime, you're going to need clothes."

"I've got clothes."

"Not for skiing."

"No, you're right." My leather jacket and motorcycle boots really wouldn't cut it.

"I'll have some brought to you. In the meantime, I'll get you the other suite on this floor."

"I can go home tonight."

"It will be easier if you were here. I insist."

There was a hardness to his voice that made me nervous. He clearly didn't want to let me out of his sight, which meant he was still mega suspicious of me.

Was I really going to do this?

Yes.

My father's old mob buddy had almost strangled me to death and had threatened to do the same to my friend. That was all the motivation I needed. Whatever happened, I could use the money Garreth Locke paid me and take the opportunity to find the book to save Meg.

"So, what now?" I asked.

"Just a moment." He went to the phone on the table by the couch and called down to the desk. Within thirty seconds, he'd gotten their agreement to give him the other penthouse. When he hung up, he turned to me. "It's done."

"You didn't tell them it was me staying there." For which I was immensely grateful. My colleagues would not understand why I was suddenly staying in the top floor penthouse. As much as I might like to have a rags-to-riches Cinderella story, that kind of thing didn't happen to girls like me. "Will they bring a key up?"

"They're on their way. In a minute, you can go over and get settled in."

"And out of your hair."

He smiled, but again, it didn't reach his eyes.

There was a quiet knock on the door.

"That will be them," he said. "Go on. I'll have dinner sent to your room."

My stomach rumbled in response. It had been a while since I'd eaten, and I was suddenly famished. "All right. Thanks."

He nodded and stepped aside. I walked past him, keeping as much space between us as possible. Still, I caught the scent of him—the forest and rain, a divine aroma that made my heart race, and I held my breath to avoid drawing more of it into my lungs. There was something about him that was magnetic. He made me feel like a smaller planet orbiting a sun, and I hated it.

I reached the door and found his two companions on the other side. Their faces were impassive as they met my gaze, and I wondered if they'd been able to hear our conversation through the door.

Nah. It was incredibly thick wood.

Still, I glimpsed knowledge in their gazes as they looked at me, and I didn't like it.

Fortunately, they stepped aside to let me pass and I was inside the other suite within seconds. There were only three on this floor, which meant his companions had to be sharing the other one.

I shut the door and leaned against it with a sigh.

What the hell had just happened?

Yes, I'd been caught. But now I was staying in the other penthouse suite, about to go on a skiing weekend as some kind of spy?

Wearily, I scrubbed my hand over my face. How was this now my life?

Prior to this, it had been an endless cycle of work and ramen noodles, occasionally punctuated by breaks to fix my finicky motorcycle.

I shook the thoughts away. No point dwelling on them. To survive, I had to keep moving forward and adjust. I'd learned that quickly enough after my mother had died.

And anyway, how often did I get to be a guest in a hotel room like this?

Never.

I opened my eyes, and excitement fluttered through me. The suite was just as big and beautiful as Garreth Locke's had been, but the colors were softer, a muted blue. The view from the windows was spectacular, but before checking it out, I turned to look out the peephole into the hallway.

Immediately, I spotted one of Garreth Locke's companions standing in the hallway. Arms crossed over his chest, his stony gaze was glued to my door.

Yep. A guard. Just as I'd thought.

No matter. If I wanted to escape, I'd go out the

Midnight Moon

window. I strode over to admire the magnificent view. From up here, I could see the street below, then the water beyond. It glittered enticingly, though I knew it had to be frigid.

I turned my attention to the street to see if anyone was out and spotted the woman who'd been with Garreth Locke earlier tonight. She stood in the recessed doorway of a bar, a warm coat bundled up to her neck as she watched my windows.

Shit.

He'd put a guard on the outside of the building, too. Which meant he knew how I'd sneaked in. I hadn't seen anyone when I'd first made the climb, but there were quite a few places they could have hidden. They weren't hiding anymore. They were out in the open, making it clear that I shouldn't try to run for it.

A chill raced over me. What else did he know about me?

Hopefully, nothing. My footprint was small.

A knock sounded at the door, and I turned to answer it. The man on the other side wore the uniform of the waitstaff and carried a silver-domed tray, though I didn't know his name. I'd seen him a few times in passing, but we'd never spoken. His eyes widened as he took in my uniform.

"You can put it on the table, thanks." I gestured toward the table in front of the window.

He nodded and strode forward, placing the tray

down and removing the dome to reveal a massive spread of food. He was out the door before I could even ask about the bill, shutting it silently behind him.

Surprise made my head spin as I approached the tray. It was covered in the most delectable assortment of seafood I'd ever seen. Lobster, shrimp, crab, and scallops. Along with a beautiful salad and basket of fancy bread. A bottle of wine sat next to it, and not the kind in a box, either. This was way nicer than anything I ever bought.

"What the hell?" I muttered as I picked up one of the crusty rolls and shoved it in my mouth. I hadn't eaten anything besides ramen and baloney sandwiches for months while I saved up for school, and this was decadent.

Maybe Garreth Locke was just rubbing in the fact that he was wealthy and well connected, but I didn't mind. Hell, if I got to eat like this all weekend, I'd volunteer to be his spy for even longer.

The next thirty minutes passed like a dream as I gorged myself on the food. I ate way too much, but it was impossible to stop, especially when I saw the chocolate cake under the tiny silver dome on the desert tray.

I'd just finished when another knock sounded at the door.

As I made my way over, I wished I were wearing my own clothes. It was weird as hell to be a guest in the nicest suite while wearing my housekeeping uniform.

Midnight Moon

I peeked through the peephole, but something big and blue blocked it. Frowning, I opened the door to find a clothing rack stuffed with clothes. A small woman stood next to it.

Her eyes brightened as she spotted me, and she grinned widely. "You must be Lyra."

"I am." How the hell did she know my name?

"I'm Bella." She stuck out her hand and I shook it, taking in her sleek blond hair and bright blue eyes. She wore a matching blue jumpsuit that had to be silk. Despite the towering stilettos she wore, she was barely five feet tall. "Let's get you dressed!"

I stepped back as she shoved the clothing rack inside the room, my gaze running over the beautiful fabrics and colors. I wasn't one for fashion, sticking mostly to beat-up jeans and old T-shirts, but maybe that was because I'd never had any money. Faced with such a jackpot, my heart raced.

"What's going on?" I asked.

"Garreth Locke has ordered a full wardrobe for you." She turned and grinned, her smile even wider than it had been. "Which is *super* exciting. Having a man buy all your clothes." She made a fainting gesture.

"I'd rather have a check." I gestured to the fabrics. "He's paying?"

"Of course. So don't be shy. I've got quite the assortment here." She pulled off a luxurious looking ivory sweater and shoved it at me. "This, for example, would be great around the fireplace on a cold winter night."

I took the sweater and nearly swooned at the soft texture of the wool. Cashmere? I had no idea what the fanciest yarn was, but this was surely it. "It feels like a cloud."

"Try it on."

I peeked at the price tag as I pulled it off the hanger and nearly passed out. Eight hundred dollars. Unable to help myself, I squeaked, "What the hell!"

"I know, right?" Bella nodded. "Crazy expensive, but he can afford it."

"Yeah." I breathed out the word, stunned as I donned the sweater over my uniform.

"That won't do!" Bella waved her hands. "Strip! You need to see how the lines really work."

The next hour flew by as Bella tossed garments at me to try. By the time we were done, I had new sweaters, jeans, boots, and snow gear. First lobster and champagne, and now an epic personalized shopping spree?

It was enough to throw me totally off my game.

That's it.

Garreth Locke had to be playing some kind of crazy mind game with me, because this was *not* normal.

"Do rich people really live like this?" I asked Bella.

She shrugged. "Some do. It's crazy what you see in a job like mine." She packed up the clothes that hadn't

Midnight Moon

worked and headed toward the door. "Enjoy it, though. Lord knows, I'd kill to be you."

"Ha." I gave a weak laugh and waved goodbye as she left the room, then headed for the bathroom. A hot shower would clear my head, right?

It didn't, but at least I had the best shower of my life in the massive marble room. By the time I laid down in the cloud-like bed, I was exhausted.

"What the hell is going on?" I whispered to the ceiling. Even though I'd agreed to this—it played into my plans and everything—I had definitely lost my footing.

Garreth Locke is on the other side of this wall.

The thought jumped into my head. The layout of the rooms was identical, which meant his bedroom was directly on the other side of this wall, with his bed pressed against it.

Memories of the moment he'd me pinned against the wall filled my head, and heat flushed through me.

As I lay in bed, the sound of voices caught my attention. Were they coming from Garreth's suite? Definitely.

At first, I couldn't make out the words. But my curiosity got the better of me and I climbed up to press my ear to the wall. My hearing had always been freakishly good, and with a little concentration, I could make out what they were saying.

"He's a problem, I'm telling you." The voice that filtered through wall wasn't recognizable, but the next one was.

"I know," Garreth said. "We'll try it my way, but if he really is deceiving us, we'll kill him."

I gasped.

Kill him?

Oh, shit.

Who were they talking about?

My father's stories of his time in the mob—and the one about Garreth in particular—resurfaced.

He really was a killer. And he didn't tolerate deceit, that was for sure.

I swallowed hard, fear icing my veins.

I was deceiving him. I'd already lied plenty in our short meeting.

I could never let him know.

8

Garreth

The next morning, I waited for Lyra in the lobby. The night had been...slow.

After Seth had finished warning me about Sam Montblake and the City Pack, he had left my room. I'd tried to sleep, but the knowledge that my mate was within a few feet of me had kept me awake far too long. Despite my conviction that she would be bad for the pack, I still wanted her. I couldn't help myself.

Disgusted, I stared up at the ceiling. Had it been overkill to send her clothing last night? And the food? It had been excessive for anyone's needs, but when it came time to show restraint where she was concerned, I'd found it to be impossible. Hell, I'd even had a full buffet spread sent to her room for breakfast.

It had been less than twenty-four hours and I was already losing it over her. How had this happened so quickly? I was turning into my father, putting my own desires before the needs of the pack. Before duty and the promise I'd made in his memory. I needed to put them first, to fix what he had broken.

When Lyra appeared on the other side of the lobby, I smelled her before I saw her. The divine scent of lavender, honey, and a fresh breeze caught my attention, and that of my wolf. A low growl of desire rose in my throat, and I bit it back, even more disgusted with myself.

As she approached, I schooled my features into blankness, though it was a struggle. She looked beautiful, her dark hair waving down her back and her eyes glowing golden. She wore a soft white sweater and dark jeans, along with tall leather boots. They were nice enough clothes, but I'd thought her just as beautiful in her housekeeping uniform.

She stopped in front of me. "Good morning."

I grunted back, wanting to keep my distance.

"All right, then." She raised her brows. "Someone needs another coffee."

"I'm fine. Are you ready?"

She gestured to the luggage boy ten feet behind her, holding her new bags. "Evan has my things."

"Evan?"

Midnight Moon

"I work here, remember? So, I know the staff." She looked around, clearly uncomfortable. "Speaking of which, it's weird to be on this side of things, so let's get the hell out of here before I'm the subject of too much gossip."

"Gossip?"

"Among the staff. I have a life here, you know. And the fact that I'm suddenly with you and dressed like this is going to make people wonder if I'm an escort. Which is fine and all, but I don't want to deal with the looks the dudes will send me."

I grimaced. "They could just think you're my date."

"Us? Together?" She laughed. "No one would buy it. Guys like you don't go for housekeepers."

"You don't know anything about me."

"You going to prove me wrong?"

"No." My tone was too sharp, but we were getting dangerously close to talking about relationships, and I couldn't have that. "Let's go."

I headed toward the front of the hotel, where my vehicle waited. Seth, my beta, had already left for the gathering at the ski resort, and Lyra and I would take my car.

She kept pace by my side as we strode to the hotel's front doors. They whooshed open as we drew near, and the valet stepped up to hand me my keys. I tipped him and nodded my thanks.

Unconsciously, I moved to open the passenger door

for Lyra, but the valet beat me to it. Good. I didn't need to get into the habit of doing such things.

As I settled in behind the wheel of the vehicle, I couldn't help but look at Lyra. Seatbelt buckled, she stared stoically forward, as if we were headed to the guillotine.

"Was your night all right?" I asked as I pulled out into traffic.

"Crazy, but fine."

"Crazy?"

"The way you people live is insane. You had a store sent to my room."

"Ah, that." The pack hadn't always had money, so I understood. We'd struggled financially when I'd been growing up. Fortunately, I'd found I had a knack for investing and our fortunes had turned around. But I still remembered what it was like to be poor.

"Anyway, thanks," she said.

"Sure."

We rode in silence as we left town, the tension tightening the air between us. The near kiss we'd shared last night had rolled over and over in my mind, haunting my every waking moment. Now that I was alone with her, it was all I could think about.

"So, we're going skiing." Apprehension and doubt echoed in her voice.

"It will be fine," I said. "The weekend will be quick. And if you don't want to ski, you don't have to."

"I will. And otherwise, you just want me to listen to conversations and see if they're talking behind your back?"

"That would be good, though I doubt they'd let you hear anything incriminating. Your primary goal will be to make yourself present wherever they are. If they approach you and try to get you to interfere on their behalf, let me know."

"That seems unlikely."

"You don't know them."

"Fair enough."

As we climbed into the snowy mountains, my curiosity got the better of me. "What are you?"

"Um, a housekeeper. I thought you knew that."

I frowned. "Playing it close to the vest. All right."

"Um, I guess?"

That didn't make much sense, but I didn't push her. My best chance at keeping my distance was to know as little as possible about her.

Lyra

The ride through the mountains was beautiful, albeit strange. Some of the things that Garreth Locke said made no sense, but who was I to unravel the eccentricities of the insanely wealthy?

By the time we arrived at a massive stone and iron gate, I was ready to get out of the car. The tension of being so close to him was beginning to wear me out, and I needed to be alone.

"Is this a private residence?" I asked as the car climbed the steep path through the forest. Huge trees towered on either side of the drive, heavily laden with fluffy white snow. The day was sunny and the sky brilliantly blue above, and it was like entering a winter wonderland.

"It is. Owned by the Cascade Pack. They've hosted the gathering for years."

He kept talking about packs. Or was it PAC? Didn't that stand for political action committee? That's what it had to be.

"What kind of business are you in anyway?" I wanted more specifics.

"Investing. But that's not why we're here."

"Why are—" I cut off when the building appeared through the trees. The massive wooden structure took my breath away. I'd never seen anything so beautiful in all my life. It looked like the most perfect mountaintop chalet I'd ever seen—a structure more suited to old Europe than America. Not that I'd ever seen a chalet in real life, but this place gave fairytales a run for their money.

Midnight Moon

And yet there was something intrinsically American about the place as well. Perhaps it was the sheer size of it, or the huge wooden planks that covered parts of the house. Evergreen boughs decorated the windowsills, even though Christmas had passed, and beautiful trees sparkled with twinkling lights, despite the bright sun.

"Wow," I breathed. "Someone actually *lives* here?"

"Quite a few someones."

"I'd have a big family, too, if I lived in a place like this." Envy wasn't one of my normal emotions, but it was hard not to be a little wistful when looking at the house. It was truly magnificent.

Garreth pulled the car around to the front. The massive front doors were beautiful, the most beautiful doors I'd ever seen, made of wood and glass, and designed to look like two huge pine trees. They were protected by a wooden overhang draped with fragrant evergreen and twinkle lights, and for the briefest moment, I felt like I'd entered a dream.

The huge doors swung open, and two men came out. They were both dressed in simple dark clothing with name badges pinned to their shirts.

Wow. Staff in a house. This was the big leagues.

"Our bags are in the back," Garreth said as he walked around the front of the car and handed one of the men the keys. "Where is everyone?"

"They should be coming down to meet you, sir."

"Thank you."

Garreth joined me and held out an arm. I stared at it, hesitating at first.

"We're supposed to pretend to be a couple, remember."

"Right." I slipped my hand into the crook of his arm, shivering at the warmth beneath my palm.

For his part, Garreth hardly seemed to notice me. He strode toward the doors, and I had to pick up the pace to keep up.

As we entered the magnificent foyer with a huge fireplace at one end, my gaze was drawn to the sweeping staircase that arced around the left side of the room. More evergreen hung from the wooden banister, smelling deliciously of the forest.

A small group of figures appeared at the top of the stairs. I looked up at them, and it took everything I had to stifle my gasp.

I didn't recognize three of them, but the one in the front was from the freaking *mob*, the same man who'd strangled me In my apartment. He strode down the stairs like he owned the place. And instead of a fancy suit, he was wearing jeans and an expensive-looking sweater.

Cold fear iced my spine.

What the hell was going on?

I wasn't surprised the mob was involved with politics, but I hadn't seen this coming.

When his gaze landed on me, his eyes narrowed

briefly. I gave him the slightest shake of my head—more of a twitch than anything else—and he seemed to get the picture. Hopefully.

Hell, *I* barely got the picture, but I figured out in a split second the importance of keeping everything a secret. The creepy mobster seemed to agree, because as he stepped onto the first floor, he asked, "And who is your guest, Garreth?"

"My new...friend." The way he said friend made it sound like there was a hell of a lot more between us, and the mobster's eyebrows rose.

"Really?"

Garreth smiled, though it didn't reach his eyes. "Really."

The man smiled back without warmth.

Holy tits. Garreth Locke wanted me to find out if this guy would try to recruit me—*and he already had.*

Should I confess?

No. The conversation I'd heard last night proved that Garreth wouldn't tolerate lies. I'd learned from my father that you couldn't trust others, especially men like Garreth.

I could trust only myself. I drew in a deep breath and tried to calm my racing heart.

The leader reached out a hand to me. "I'm Sam Montblake. City PAC."

I held out my hand, trying to keep it from visibly shaking. "I'm Lyra. Nice to meet you."

He introduced the three others—two women and a man—as belonging to different PACs. I wasn't surprised to hear that Garreth and Montblake were both involved in politics—the mob often was. But were these other individuals criminals as well? Or did they have no idea who they were dealing with?

He looked toward Garreth. "You've missed lunch, but you're just in time for skiing. Ready to hit the slopes?"

Hit the slopes?

Since when did the mob *hit the slopes?*

I was in the twilight zone.

"Of course." The edge in Garreth's voice suggested he wasn't that into skiing, but he'd do it anyway.

"Excellent. After you change, we'll meet you out front and ride up to the top of the mountain together."

Garreth nodded, then took my hand and strode toward the stairs. The staff followed us with the bags, and I didn't dare look back at the bastard who was forcing me into this situation.

When we reached the top floor, it was suddenly much quieter and cozier. The two staff members led the way, and Gareth hung back a few steps to give us privacy.

"Why did you say yes if you clearly don't want to go skiing?" I asked.

"This weekend isn't about what I want. It's about learning to trust each other in the deal we're trying to broker."

Midnight Moon

"Which is?"

"We both want a piece of land very much. I own it, but they're threatening to take it. I could fight them for it, but I'd rather try a new form of shifter diplomacy."

"What is shifter diplomacy?"

He gave me a perplexed look, as if I were simple. "What don't you understand? It's self-explanatory. Shifter. Diplomacy."

"Still not getting it." But he was acting like I should, which made me feel a bit dumb. What the hell was *shifter*?

"Then you don't need to understand. You just need to do what I tell you."

Well, now I felt dumb and annoyed. Hurt streaked through me, leaving razor blade cuts where it brushed against my heart.

We reached the staff member who waited by a tall wooden doorway. The man gestured inside, and we proceeded him into the room. Garreth entered first, his gaze moving quickly left and right. He was inspecting the room for threats, a precaution I recognized. I'd used the same tactics back in my thieving youth.

When he seemed satisfied that it was safe, he allowed me to follow him inside.

What I saw took my breath away. The massive room had a high vaulted ceiling supported by large oak beams. Glass doors led to a large patio with a glorious view over the snowy mountains beyond. A fireplace big enough to stand in sat along one wall, with the huge bed opposite. The bed resembled a blue velvet lake, heavy draperies hanging from the wooden posters.

Outside, fat puffs of snow began to fall.

"It's like a winter fantasy," I murmured.

He just shrugged.

"That's all you've got, a shrug?"

He said nothing as he took his bag from the side of the door where the staff member had put it and headed toward the bathroom. As he disappeared through the door, I shouted after him. "Are you trying to be a dick, or does it just come natural?"

"Natural."

9

Garreth

I shut the bathroom door and leaned against it, staring up at the ceiling as I took a deep breath.

Seeing Lyra near the City Pack alpha had been enough to send my protective instincts into overdrive. When he'd stepped close to her, it had taken all my control not to growl and declare *mine.*

And that car ride.

Fates. I dragged a hand over my face, trying to forget how intoxicating it had been to sit next to her for so long.

I knew what I had to do. So why couldn't I do it?

Keeping my distance from her was proving harder with every minute. I couldn't even guarantee I'd have the self-control to continue this charade, something entirely unheard of for me.

There was only one option—be a bastard so that she didn't want to be anywhere near me.

She thought I was a dick, so that was a good start. She'd go running from me when this weekend was over if I could just keep that up. Good thing it came naturally.

But first, I needed to figure out why she'd been in my room. It was a shame I needed to go skiing. Not that this weekend was about enjoyment.

The skiing was a tradition—a way to prove our strength and bravery in our human forms before we shifted later.

I changed into ski clothes as quickly as I could. I didn't ski much in my regular life, but I'd become used to this challenge over the years. With any luck, Sam Montblake would take the worst of what was coming on the slopes.

It would also be a good opportunity to determine what species Lyra was. Shifter? Witch? Not a vampire, though they could walk in the daylight. She didn't have the teeth for it.

I dressed and returned to the room.

As soon as I stepped through the door, I spotted her. She stood in a beam of warm golden sunlight, her shirt raised over her head as she pulled on a ski jumper. For

Midnight Moon

the briefest moment, I caught a glimpse of a silky bra and smooth skin.

My heart went into overdrive and heat streaked through me, straight to my cock. I spun around, knowing that every second I looked at her threatened my self-control. I'd keep a handle on it—I wasn't an animal, despite my shifter nature—but I didn't like wanting her.

"How long were you standing there?" Suspicion echoed in her voice.

"Are you dressed now?"

"Yes."

"Good." I turned back around. She was fully dressed in black ski clothes. Breathing a sigh of relief, I said, "Let's go."

"You're not going to apologize for barging in on me?"

"It's my room."

"Mine too. Dick."

I felt a smile tug at the corner of my mouth. Being a bastard was working well. She was so easily riled, I'd have her running off in no time. "Let's go. They'll be waiting for us."

"Fine. Is there anything specific you want me to do while we ski?"

"I'm not sure you should ski. It could be dangerous."

"I'll be fine."

"You've heard what happens on these slopes?"

"Yep. Looking forward to it."

Her call. "All right, then. Just focus on staying upright, but if Sam Montblake tries to dig for information about me, let me know."

"Sure. But I still don't see how skiing is going to help you broker whatever deal you want."

"You'll see."

As expected, the other alphas were waiting outside near two large black SUVs. Some had brought their mates, though not all.

We climbed into the back of one of the vehicles. It felt like a damned organized school trip, until the bastard in the passenger seat looked at me and said with a straight face, "You're dead meat."

"We'll see about that." I sensed Lyra's confused gaze on me but didn't turn my head. She'd said she knew what the skiing was like up here, but, apparently, she hadn't been aware of the competitive aspect. Not only were the slopes full of dangerous obstacles, but the competitors tried to take each other out to ensure their pack made it to the bottom first.

The driver glanced back at Lyra. "So, what are you?"

"Gemini. Housekeeper. Motorcycle enthusiast."

"That's not what I meant. But motorcycle enthusiast?" Interest perked in his voice.

"Yeah."

Midnight Moon 99

Lyra

Before I could say any more about myself, the vehicle turned off the main road and bumped along a well-worn path through the snow. It looked like it wasn't an official road, and it was a damned good thing this car was built like a tank. I had to grab the overhead handle to keep myself from sliding into Garreth, and the conversation quieted as we approached the top of the mountain.

When the vehicle finally pulled to a stop, I was more than ready to get the hell out of there. The tension in the tiny compartment was enough to drive a monk batty, and I was desperate to breathe the fresh air.

Everyone else seemed to feel the same way because they climbed quickly out of the car. I jumped down into the thick snow, grateful for my new ski boots. The morning was cold and bright, still as a placid lake. Massive trees towered around us, piled high with snow that didn't shift or fall in the calm air.

I dragged a cold breath into my lungs, loving the fresh scent of the trees. I'd always had an unusually strong sense of smell, and this place was absolutely divine. I'd never been anywhere as remote or beautiful —spent my whole life in the city, in fact.

People around us were gathering ski equipment from the backs of the vehicles and snapping on skis.

Garreth collected ours, then nodded for me to follow him toward the edge of the slope.

I trudged through the snow after him, pulling up the zipper of the jacket and tugging my hat down over my head. My breath puffed out in white clouds, and the sun sparkled off the snow.

"This is gorgeous." I stopped next to Garreth.

He was staring down the slope, so I joined him, following his gaze.

"Holy shit," I murmured.

It was steep as hell and covered in trees and mounds of snow.

"Are you sure about this?" he asked.

"Yeah." *Nope.* But no way I was going to admit to that. "I'm athletic and good on my feet. I'll be fine." The first part, at least, was true. Being fine?

Still to be determined.

"All right. But you can opt out if you want."

"Give me the skis." I stuck out a hand, and he passed them over.

It took me a minute to sort out my equipment, and Garreth ended up kneeling at my feet to adjust my skis. He seemed annoyed about it, but he did it.

"You sure you can do this?" he asked.

"Yeah. Don't worry about me, I've got this."

"All right." He finished fiddling with the bindings and stood.

"Thanks."

Midnight Moon

He grunted and put on his own equipment.

"Everyone ready?" A voice shouted from the sidelines. I looked over and spotted a woman standing on a small pile of snow. She looked strong and capable, her face weathered and wise.

At least a dozen people shouted that they were, and the rest joined in a minute later.

"First to the bottom wins," she shouted. "No rules besides no killing."

No killing?

Wide-eyed, I looked at Garreth, but he didn't notice. His gaze was on Sam Montblake, who was watching us.

Jesus, what the hell was going on here?

"On your mark, go!" The woman's voice triggered an explosion of movement.

Skiers took off, hurtling down the mountain. I followed Garreth, determined not to be left behind. As I hurtled down the mountain and the snow zipped beneath my skis, my heart lunged into my throat.

One thought echoed in my head—*I'm gonna die.*

The world was moving by at sixty miles an hour, and it was all I could do to stay on my feet.

Maybe I'd been a little overconfident.

Garreth went ahead of me, making sure to pick a path that avoided the worst of the moguls and trees. I followed, my cheeks prickling from the cold as my heart hammered inside my chest.

Out of the corner of my eye, I saw a tree appear out

of nowhere. A man slammed into it with a sickening thud, but I was past him before I had time to see if he was okay, zipping down the mountain, barely in control.

More moguls appeared, dotting the space between the trees. Garreth took a few of them, but I went around, slowly getting the hang of navigating on skis. Thank God for my freakish physical aptitude.

All around us, skiers zipped through the trees. I watched one guy slam into another skier, taking him down and continuing down the mountain.

Holy shit, he'd levelled that guy out on purpose.

A minute later, I saw another woman ski so close to a guy that she forced him to slam into a branch. He went down, and she gave a war cry of victory.

Oh, my God, these people were crazy.

My heart thundered as I looked around, trying to spot any oncoming attacks. Apparently, I didn't just need to worry about trees and moguls—the other skiers were the biggest threat.

When we reached the thickest part of the forest, I spotted a man beelining for me.

Shit. I might be able to ski, but there was no way I could take him out and stay upright. I was barely holding onto my footing as it was.

I navigated to the right, trying to outrun him. Another skier cut me off, forcing me over a mogul, and I went flying through the air like a terrified chicken.

I landed hard, barely keeping my footing.

The man had followed me over the mogul and had nearly reached me. Fear cleared my thoughts and cooled my nerves. I crouched low for the best aerodynamics and went for speed.

It wasn't enough.

He was too fast, nearly to me, a vicious glint in his eye. The trees were closing in, and I realized his plan.

Shove me into a tree like those other poor bastards.

I'd never survive that. I darted right, narrowly avoiding his attack just as Garreth slammed into him and threw him into a tree. I was so distracted that I hit an unseen bump in the snow and went sailing.

I landed hard on my butt. Dazed, I stared forward at the blinding whiteness. Garreth crouched in front of me.

"Are you all right?" Concern creased his brow.

"I'm good. Thanks for getting him."

He nodded and pulled me to my feet. "I've got your back."

I've got your back.

It sounded nice. Really nice.

Maybe he wasn't so bad. He'd gotten that bastard off my back, after all. And he seemed really worried about me right now.

No. I couldn't rely on it. You could never rely on that kind of thing. So, I didn't say anything more.

"Ready to keep going?"

"I guess."

"You've got this."

"Sure." I set off down the slope, focusing on the path in front of me. Garreth stuck by my side as we cut through the cold winter air. Adrenaline sang through my veins, keeping me sharp.

Soon, a barricade of trees appeared in front of us. There were so damned many, and they seemed to be *moving.* Like this was a real-life video game or something.

Shit, was I hallucinating?

Because this was crazy.

We reached the tree line, and a thick fog descended. I couldn't see in front of me, and fear clutched at my heart.

"Follow the sound of my skis!" Garreth shouted.

I could barely pick up the swoosh of his skis, and I navigated to them. Thank God for my excellent hearing. Pine needles brushed against my face as I whipped past hidden trees, scaring the hell out of me.

By the time we burst from the cloud bank and forest, I was nearly hyperventilating.

I caught sight of Sam Montblake. He seemed to be gunning for Garreth, ahead of me.

"Garreth!" I shouted. "From behind!"

He looked back and spotted Montblake. The other man put more speed into his effort, pushing himself even faster down the mountain. Garreth took advantage of a mogul, flying up and over the white mound. When

Midnight Moon

he landed, he aimed for Montblake, managing to knock him over into the snow.

As I flew by the downed man, I heard his growl.

Serves you right.

I loved seeing him on his ass like an idiot.

By the time we reached the bottom, there were only about six competitors left on their feet. Everyone was standing in front of a small cafe that had been built at the base of the slope, grinning, and smiling at each other.

I managed to stop without falling, then leaned over and propped my hands on my knees. Nausea roiled in my stomach, and I breathed deeply, trying not to puke.

I'd nearly died.

A few times.

"Are you all right?" Garreth's voice sounded at my side, and I looked up.

"All right?" I straightened. "You people are insane."

All around, the fallen competitors were arriving. Many were covered in snow and looked like they'd been through the ringer, but no one looked grievously wounded. When I saw the guy who'd slammed into the tree, my jaw dropped.

"Shouldn't he be dead?" I asked.

Garreth frowned, but before he could answer, his gaze landed on someone behind me. It narrowed slightly, then cleared. "Why don't I get you a coffee while you talk to Montblake?"

I looked back and spotted the mob boss striding toward us, his skis tucked under his arm. He appeared no worse for the fall he'd taken, although he did look mildly annoyed.

"Time to get to work, got it." I nodded at Garreth. "But I don't like coffee. Hot chocolate, please."

"Coming right up."

The idea that I was going to do something as silly as drink a hot chocolate after barely surviving murder skiing was a bit nuts, but that didn't even scratch the surface. I was about to be a double agent at a weird political gathering.

Montblake stopped in front of me, but before he could speak, I demanded. "What the hell are you doing here?"

"I could ask the same of you."

"Trying to do what you told me." I lowered my voice until it was nearly inaudible, though Garreth was inside the little coffee shop. "I broke into his hotel suite, but the book was gone."

"So now you're here, posing as his girlfriend?"

"Pretty much. I knew I needed a second shot at getting that damned book. But I don't understand why you're making me do it if you were going to be spending the damned weekend with him."

His brows rose, and an incredulous glint entered his eyes. "Here? You expect me steal from him at a gathering of the packs? They'd tear me apart if I were caught."

Midnight Moon

"Oh, great. So, I can look forward to being torn apart?" Prior to the skiing, I'd have thought that was a euphemism, but now I wasn't so sure. "Is this deadly?"

"Of course, it is." His eyes turned cold. "Because I'll kill you if you don't succeed."

I swallowed hard, believing him wholeheartedly.

"Why did he really bring you?" Montblake demanded.

No way in hell would I tell him the truth. Not out of loyalty to Garreth—I felt loyalty only to myself. Trusted only myself. And that's why I'd keep all info close to the vest until I knew what to do with it.

"He caught me in his room, and I said I was the housekeeper. I think he believed me. Turns out, he had the hots for me and invited me here."

"Hmm." Montblake nodded knowingly, and he appeared to be believing it. Too easily. I was attractive, but I wasn't that hot. And yet, he bought it totally.

Weird.

"Delivery." Garreth's voice sounded from a distance, and I turned to see him carrying a paper coffee cup toward me. He nodded at Montblake, who nodded back, then handed me the cup. "Shall we meet the others at the vehicles? It looks like they're ready to head back."

The group was loading their equipment into the trunks of the SUVs, and I followed Garreth toward them. He put our stuff in the trunk, then joined me in the backseat. I sipped the hot chocolate, delighted with the quality. It was rich and dark. Glorious.

Soon, we were driving back to the house. The group sat in silence, which I was grateful for, but when the car stopped in the middle of the forest, I frowned.

"What's going on?" I asked.

Up ahead, all the other cars had stopped as well.

Montblake glanced back. "We're back on pack property, so we'll take the scenic way home."

I looked out the window. "More scenic than this?"

He just grinned and climbed out. Before he shut the door behind him, he said, "We like to take advantage of having no humans around."

"Humans? That's a weird way to put it," I said.

"What would you call them?" he asked.

"Uh, people?"

He shrugged and turned away, striding toward the trees where half of the skiers waited. The driver turned to me and Garreth. "One of you mind driving back so I can join him? Unless you want to go with them?"

They were going to walk all the way back through the snow? "I'm good. I'll drive."

"You?" The driver asked Garreth. "Coming with?"

"I'll stay with her."

The man climbed out of the seat, and I moved around to the front. As I was about to climb into the driver's seat, I caught a flash of colorful light near the trees.

Midnight Moon

I leaned around the hood of the car and spotted Montblake. A dark gray cloud swirled around him. A split second later, the mist faded, and he'd transformed into a massive mountain lion.

Shock lanced me. "What the…"

Three more figures were surrounded by light of different colors-red, blue, and silver. A moment later, they turned into animals. Two wolves and a bear.

I stumbled backward, my heart racing.

What the hell was I seeing?

There was no way this was real.

10

Lyra

Panic exploded inside my chest. Garreth had drugged the hot chocolate, that was it. That's why I was seeing people turn into animals.

"Lyra?" Concern echoed in Garreth's voice. "Are you all right?"

I blinked and looked over at him. Confusion flashed on his face. "What's going on with you? It's like you've seen a ghost."

"Did you drug the hot chocolate?" My voice was high with hysteria.

He looked toward the other vehicles, as if concerned they might hear. The cars were already pulling away and heading up the road, so no help was coming from that quarter.

"Oh, my God, you did." I stumbled back in the snow.

"Get in the car." His voice was low with warning.

Behind him, near the tree line, the rest of the people transformed into animals and loped off into the forest.

Holy shit, was it normal to have the same hallucination repeatedly? Because I refused to believe this was real. It was just too crazy.

"I'm not getting in that car with you," I said.

"Yes, you are. I don't know why you're suddenly losing your senses."

"I just saw people turn into animals. It's more than losing my senses."

"Of course, you saw them turn into animals. They're shifters."

"Shifters. That's the word you used before."

"I don't remember, but I'm sure I did." He gripped my arm. "Come on, get in the car."

"No!" I jerked free of his grasp and looked back toward the trees.

All of the people—animals—were gone, and it was easy to believe that I'd imagined it. I was desperate to believe I'd imagined it.

Shock flashed on Garreth's face, and when he spoke, his voice was slow. "Lyra, you do know that shifters are real, don't you?"

"Are you insane?"

"What about magic?"

"Double insane, I knew it." How the hell was I going to get away from him? "You're crazy, and you've drugged me. That explains it."

"I didn't. I'll take you back to the coffee shop and you can ask the barista if there's anything strange in your drink."

He sounded confident, but it only heightened my panic. I'd rather have drugged hot chocolate than be hallucinating.

"Holy fates." He dragged a hand through his hair, appearing utterly perplexed. "You were acting a bit strange, but I didn't realize why. You have no idea magic exists."

"How the hell was I supposed to know that?" I held up my hands. "*Not* that I believe you."

"You're going to have to, because it's real."

I walked to the car and leaned against it before my legs gave out. I squeezed my eyes shut and recalled the vision of the people turning into animals. I thumped my head against the car and muttered, "I can't believe they did that."

"We're away from humans. It's fine."

"Away from humans? That's what you're concerned about? Not the fact that he turned into a giant mountain lion."

"Of course, I'm concerned about humans."

"You say it like you're not one of them." Horrified

understanding dawned. "Hang on. Are *you* one of them?"

"A mountain lion?" Disgust echoed in his voice. "No."

"Whew."

"I'm a wolf."

"Fucking fantastic." My knees gave out, and I sank to the ground in the snow. Maybe I should be running, but I believed him. I believed what I'd seen. Which meant that if I ran through this forest, he would catch me. There was no way I could outrun a wolf.

I looked up at him towering over me, handsome and broad.

"Are you like a scary humanoid wolf on two legs or an animal wolf?"

"Animal. Just a bit bigger than the ones you'd find in the wild."

"Holy shit." My voice sounded dazed. "So, this really isn't a gathering of political action committees, is it?"

"Political action committees?" His brow furrowed.

"You kept talking about packs. At first, I thought it was a company, but then when there were multiples, I decided they were PACs. Like, the kind that try to sway elections."

He huffed out a surprised sound and dragged a hand through his hair. "Holy fates, I cannot believe this."

"Wait, why did you expect me to know about magic?" Which was *real.* I still couldn't get my mind around it. I would think I was crazy if I hadn't just seen a guy turn into a giant cat.

"Because you have some," he said. "I can smell it. Taste it."

A loud humming sounded in my head. "Nope. No way. Does not compute."

Garreth

I stared down at Lyra, who was hyperventilating in the snow. This entire endeavor had just gotten a hell of a lot more complicated.

My mate didn't know magic was real.

Didn't know that *she* was magic.

And I'd brought her to the biggest magical gathering on the west coast and expected her to act as a spy.

"Come on." Bending down, I pulled her to her feet.

She wobbled a bit unsteadily but didn't fall.

"Tell me why you thought I should know about this?"

"Let's get in the car where it's warm."

"I'm not cold."

"You're in shock."

She laughed, and it sounded slightly unhinged. "You're right, Rover."

Midnight Moon

"Rover? Are you serious? I'm a wolf, not a dog. And I'll ignore that slight to my honor, considering the shape you're in."

She laughed again, sounding even crazier, and I hauled her into my arms. With a startled yelp, she wrapped her arms around my neck. Pleasure exploded within me, along with a sense of incredible *rightness.*

I shook away the thought and carried her around the vehicle.

"What are you doing?" she breathed, her gaze so close to mine that I could see the flecks of gold in her eyes.

"Putting you in the passenger seat. You're in no condition to drive, and I can't leave you sitting in the cold."

"And *then* you'll tell me why you thought I should know about this?" There was worry in her voice, as if she already suspected she had magic.

That was a real mind fuck. People rarely made it to adulthood without recognizing their power.

I reached the other side of the car, opened the door, and settled her on the seat. Satisfied that she wasn't going to pass out on me, I shut the door and hurried to the driver's seat. When I climbed in, I didn't turn on the car.

Instead, I turned to her. "You have magic."

She thumped her head against the seat. "I thought you were going to say that."

"You don't believe me?"

She tilted her head to look at me. "Not really, no."

"But you suspected it."

She squeezed her eyes shut and tilted her face to the ceiling. "I guess it makes some kind of sense. I'm really good at climbing. Like, *way* too good. I can scale a ten-story building."

"I know. I saw you the first night you broke into my hotel."

"I was afraid of that."

I nodded. "I wanted to see what you were going to do. Instead, you ran for it. All I got was a glimpse of the edge of your skirt as you went around the corner of the building."

"Damn."

"What else can you do?" I asked.

"Crazy good hearing. And I'm naturally inclined toward anything physical. Like skiing through the deathtrap you weirdos thought was fun. Is that really enough to be magical?"

I shrugged. "It's probably not all you can do."

"What did you mean when you said you smelled and tasted my magic?"

"Every magical being has a signature that is represented by the five senses. The more powerful the being, the more signatures. The most powerful have all five."

"So, they'll smell like something, taste like something, feel like something, etc.?"

Midnight Moon

"Essentially."

"Shit. Is that why I tasted dark chocolate when I first met you? And then every time since?"

"Exactly."

"And you smell like the forest. And occasionally, silver sparkles appear around you."

I nodded. She was getting the picture. And at least she wasn't hyperventilating, anymore. She didn't mention my other two signatures—as an alpha, I had all five—but I didn't bring it up.

"What is my signature?"

"So far, I've smelled lavender, honey, and a fresh breeze. I've tasted oranges."

"Just two?"

"You could have more. You're a strange case, reaching adulthood without knowing what you are."

"Does this mean my parents were magical?"

"One of them."

She frowned. "My father."

"How do you know?"

She twitched, then shrugged. "He was weird."

It wasn't much of an answer, but I didn't push her for more.

"What next?" she asked.

"We go back to the resort. They'll be waiting for us."

"You want me to go back to a house full of monsters."

"Not monsters."

"Yet to be determined," she said.

"Either way, we go back and continue the plan."

"I'm supposed to pretend things are normal amongst a whole bunch of dangerous magical beings?"

"I'm dangerous, too."

"That doesn't make me feel better." She glared at me. "Don't forget that you're not on my side. You black-mailed me into coming here, so I don't exactly feel safe around you either."

I shifted uncomfortably. The new driving factor of my life was a desire to protect her—something that was intrinsic to being a shifter. And yet I had to resist it.

"Why don't you give me a crash course on the magical world on the drive back." She didn't sound enthusiastic, but it was a good idea.

"All right." I started the vehicle and pulled out on the road. "To begin, every magical creature you can imagine is real."

11

Lyra

As Garreth pulled up to the main house, several massive mountain lions ran out of the woods. I pressed my back against the seat, as if I could get away from them. It was a ridiculous instinct, but I couldn't help it.

"You okay?" Garreth asked.

"Fantastic." I watched as they transformed back into humans, my heartbeat thundering in my ears. Some trick of magic allowed them to keep their clothes when they changed. "Holy shit, this is insane."

"I know it's a lot to take in, and technically I'm black-mailing you to be here with me, but you can trust me to make sure you don't get hurt." There was a sincerity in his voice that caught my attention.

I turned to look at him, heartbeat still pounding. "I believe you."

Or, at least I believed that he believed it. And logically, he was probably the safest person here. He'd protected me out on the slopes.

And yet, he was a werewolf.

A freaking *werewolf.* All along he'd been a monster, and I'd had no idea.

I couldn't believe how much of my life I'd spent misunderstanding the world around me. I'd assumed Montblake and Garreth were members of rival criminal organizations because of the way my father had spoken about them, but maybe they weren't? I'd thought my mother had used the word *mob,* but she could have been mistaken, too. Maybe they lived on the other side of the law because they were shifters?

Either way, I still couldn't trust Garreth. The revelation that magic was real—that my *father* had likely been magical—was more fuel to the fire of my distrust.

Everyone lied.

I drew in a shuddery breath, feeling more alone than I ever had. More trapped.

If I was magical, I could never escape this world.

My plans for business school were more and more unlikely, but what were my alternatives?

"When I left you alone with the alpha of the City Pack, did he do or say anything suspicious?"

"Sam Montblake is the *alpha* of the City Pack, the

Midnight Moon

boss shifter?" I was still trying to wrap my head around it.

"Yes. Did he say anything?"

"He was interested in you, definitely. But he didn't say anything specific yet." I didn't feel a bit guilty about lying to him. It was a matter of survival now. I'd give him just enough info but keep my secrets safe.

I could trust only myself.

And right now, I was still planning to steal that book. It was a no-brainer. Garreth would let me go when this weekend was over, and Montblake would let me go when I handed over the book.

And anyway, it was just an object. Expensive, maybe. But not worth Meg's life.

So, there was no question what I was going to do.

"Are you ready to go in?" he asked.

"Now or never." If I sat here any longer, I could freeze in fear.

I climbed out of the car, my gaze on the mountain lions. They might have turned into people, but I could still see the shadows of beasts upon them.

Was I a shifter?

Or something else?

The mountain lions entered the house, and I prayed none of them would still be in the entry hall when I walked in. I needed a few more minutes to come to terms with their existence. Otherwise, I might look at them like they had horns and fangs.

Well, they did have fangs, at least.

Garreth led the way into the house, holding open the massive door for me as I walked inside. The main entry hall was blissfully empty. The gorgeous decor and fantasy ski-resort feeling did little to enchant me the way it first had, however.

A figure appeared at the top of the stairs, and I stiffened briefly. When they came close enough for me to recognize them, I relaxed slightly.

It was one of Garreth's people.

He strode up to us, his brow creased in concern.

"How's it going?" he asked. "Any problems out on the mountain?"

"None." Garreth turned to me. "This is Seth, my beta."

I frowned at him, unfamiliar with the term.

"Second in command."

"Ah." I nodded. "Because you're the alpha."

"You're getting the hang of it."

"Hang of what?" Seth asked, confusion on his face.

"Lyra wasn't aware that magic was real."

Seth's jaw dropped. "Holy fates, you cannot be serious."

"Oh, he is," I said.

Seth blew out a breath. "This must really screw with your head, then."

"An understatement."

He glanced up and down my body, but not in a

Midnight Moon 123

sleazy way. "I guess that means you don't know what you are, then?"

My heart dropped. "You sense that I have magic, too?"

"Yeah. Powerful magic."

Damn it, damn it, damn it.

Before I could panic, I shoved the thought from my mind and focused on the present. There were jobs to be done, and I needed to get them over with.

"What next?" I asked.

"There's a dinner party tonight," Garreth said. "If they're going to try something, it will likely be then, because the official negotiations start tomorrow."

"All right." I had a few dresses in the wardrobe he'd bought me. I wasn't usually into dresses, but that was more a matter of having no expendable income than not liking them.

"Do you have any updates?" Garreth asked Seth.

"The City Pack avoids me, especially those who defected from our pack. But within the pack, there's an unease." Seth was clearly comfortable with Garreth in a way I couldn't imagine mimicking.

Garreth frowned. "I wonder if that could work in our favor."

"Perhaps. I'd have liked the chance to talk to some of them, though."

"I'll work on that tonight," Garreth said. "In the

meantime, we need to get cleaned up. Thanks for the help."

Seth clapped a hand on Garreth's shoulder, genuine affection in his eyes. "I've got your back."

I've got your back. Just like Garreth had said to me out on the mountain. I liked the sound of it.

I felt safer not trusting anyone—how could I, after my own father had betrayed me? But damned if it wasn't lonely. My only friend was Meg, and as much as I loved her, I still couldn't get over my own issues and fully trust her. I was 95 percent the way there, but the last five percent eluded me. But this whole trust thing that Garreth had with his pack... There was something to be said for that way of life.

He's a damned werewolf.

The thought snapped me back to myself.

"Let's go get cleaned up," Garreth said.

I nodded and followed him up the stairs and down the hall. We entered our massive bedroom, and I was once again struck by how phenomenal it was. I'd never stayed in such a magnificent place, and I stopped to take it in. Focusing on something as inane as a fancy mountain resort was a lot easier than focusing on the fact that I was supposed to share a bed with a werewolf.

"You can take the shower first," Garreth said.

I nodded and strode toward the large bathroom. It, too, had a huge window overlooking the snowy moun-

Midnight Moon

tains. Double vanities were built of beautiful wood and marble, with bronze fittings shaped like tree branches.

The huge shower walls and floor were crafted from large, flat river rocks, and one wall was a glass window overlooking the mountains.

I adjusted the water to steaming, then stripped out of my clothes and climbed in. As the heat pounded on my shoulders, I stared out at the incredible view.

I could get used to this.

Nope.

I needed to get my mind away from thoughts like that. There was no way I'd ever have a chance to get used to this kind of lifestyle—even if I *did* get to go to business school like I planned. The type of money it took to build a place like this was crazy inherited wealth, not business school wealth.

I raced through the rest of my shower, wanting to give Garreth enough time that he didn't have to rush. I couldn't say that my motives were selfless, however.

I planned to use that time to search his belongings while he was in the shower.

The air was warm and fragrant as I climbed out of the shower and wrapped a towel around myself, a divine, fluffy cloud of fabric. Briefly, I considered sneaking it into my bag on the way out.

No—I wasn't a thief anymore.

Apart from trying to steal the book from Garreth,

but that was a matter of life and death. For Meg *and* for me.

I gathered up my dirty clothes and left the bathroom.

"All yours," I said, stepping into the bedroom.

Garreth turned from the mountain view, his gaze landing on me. His eyes widened, then heated. I felt my cheeks flush.

With just this towel wrapped around me, I was nearly naked.

In my rush, I'd forgotten that little tidbit.

Memories of our near kiss rushed into my mind. What would that have been like?

Incredible.

I drew in a bracing breath and headed to the other side of the room. Garreth looked away from me, but not before I got another glimpse of the heat in his eyes.

He strode to the bathroom, and I watched him go out of the corner of my vision. As soon as the door shut behind him, I leaned against the wall and breathed out.

How was it possible to have such insane chemistry with someone? I could all but *feel* his gaze on my skin like a caress, and it made my heart race and my skin heat.

And yet he was so dangerous. Too dangerous for me to get lost in daydreams of him. I needed to get dressed before I started searching for the book, and I didn't have much time.

Quickly, I began to dress. He'd sent every type of clothing imaginable to my hotel suite the other day, and the underwear that I chose was lacy and black. It felt like sin as I pulled it on, marveling at the fine workmanship.

If I could afford clothes like these, I'd definitely be way more into them.

He'd said the dinner would be semi-formal, though I didn't actually know what that meant.

I chose a short black dress, figuring that it looked formal but not stuffy. I pulled it on but couldn't reach the zipper. After a moment of struggling, I gave up and headed to Garreth's bag. I was dressed enough, and there wasn't much time left to search for the book.

As quickly as I could, I searched it, trying not to ruffle his belongings much. He was a neat packer, with carefully folded clothes in dark colors.

There was no book, however, and I frowned.

The water turned off, shocking me out of my frantic search.

I jerked backward, hurrying across the room. A moment later, Garreth opened the bathroom door. He had the fluffy white towel wrapped around his waist, revealing the broad expanse of his chest and the ridges of his abdomen. His wet hair was slicked back from his forehead, emphasizing his sharp cheekbones and brilliant eyes.

He was so phenomenally attractive that it made my head spin.

I swallowed hard and managed a weak smile, trying not to let him read my thoughts.

His gaze moved from his bag to me, as if halfway through the shower he'd realized he'd left his possessions with me, and it probably wasn't a good idea.

I tried not to look guilty, but it didn't seem to matter. When his gaze hit me, it heated again. As if unable to help himself, he glanced up and down my form. A ragged breath escaped him, and an annoyed look entered his eyes.

Annoyed at me...or annoyed with himself for clearly wanting me?

I'd never been the recipient of such obvious desire before—especially from someone who clearly didn't *want* to want me. It really screwed with my head.

Before he could remember that he was suspicious about his bag, I turned around to show him the back zipper of the dress. "Can you help me with this?"

A ragged breath escaped him, but when I turned to look at him, his expression was blank.

"Sure." He strode toward me.

I turned back around, my heartbeat pounding in my ears.

His touch was gentle and quick as he pulled the zipper up. His forest scent wrapped around me,

Midnight Moon

combining with the fragrance of the fresh soap he'd used. I wanted to inhale it forever.

When his fingertips brushed the skin of my back, I gasped.

He stepped back, and I squeezed my eyes shut, trying to get ahold of myself.

How long could we fight this?

Not long, for my part. He'd better have more self-control than me if we were going to keep this strictly business.

"I'll give you some privacy." I hurried to the bathroom and shut the door. I stared out at the snowy mountains, feeling like I needed to throw myself into the icy snowdrifts to get rid of this insane heat.

It was only a few minutes before he knocked.

I opened it, finding him dressed in a dark suit, his collar unbuttoned to reveal the strong column of his throat and the delta at the base of it. I drew in a deep, bracing breath as I looked up at him and smiled. "Ready?"

He nodded, his expression unreadable.

We left the room in silence, heading down the hall toward the main foyer.

12

Lyra

"This is just dinner?" I asked.

"Yes. Casual. A chance for everyone to catch up. There are alphas from every pack on the west coast here, and tomorrow we'll have meetings to discuss various disagreements and differences."

"That all sounds very civil."

"It isn't always. But we try."

We reached the foyer and I stopped, looking up at him. "No one is going to turn into an animal, right?"

"At dinner? Unlikely."

"Okay, good."

"I won't let anyone hurt you."

I believed him, but that didn't mean *he* wouldn't hurt

Midnight Moon 131

me. I was trying to steal from him, and he wouldn't care that I was doing it to save my friend's life. To save my own life. I'd already lied to him, and I knew what he did to liars.

As we entered the huge room, I leaned toward Garreth and whispered, "Is the City Pack the mob?"

"Not in the human sense, but they are dangerous."

"You're telling me."

His gaze sharpened. "What do you mean?"

Too late, I realized that there was a wry knowledge to my voice that suggested I knew the City Pack better than he'd expected.

"They're mountain lions." I tried to play it off, hoping he bought it.

"Hmm." He nodded, and it was impossible to say if it worked. "I'm going to go talk with some of the other alphas. Are you comfortable mingling and trying to see if they approach you?"

I nodded. "You really think they're not being honest with you, don't you?"

He shrugged. "I have good reason to."

I tried not to look guilty. "I can do it."

"Thank you. And I've got your back. If you feel uncomfortable, let me know."

I've got your back.

It was what Seth had said to him, and now he'd said it to me twice.

I liked it. A lot.

I shouldn't, but I did.

"Thanks. Now go. I'll be fine."

He strode off to join a group of men and women at the far wall. The wall itself was made entirely of glass and enormous wooden posts. Darkness had fallen, so it reflected the room, which was one of the most beautiful I'd ever seen. The wooden ceiling soared high above, supported by massive rafters that had once been huge logs. Large, rustic chandeliers hung from the beams, glittering brightly on the crowd below. Two huge fireplaces sat on opposite walls, and tables full of food and drink surrounded the people.

I made a beeline for the food as I subtly inspected the guests.

They were all magical, every single one of them able to turn into an animal.

Except me.

I shivered, pushing the thought from my mind, and focused on the spread, an amazing assortment of cheeses, meats, breads, and fruit. A plate of tiny canapés tempted me, so ornate that it seemed a shame to ruin them by shoving them in my mouth like a heathen.

I ate one, anyway, trying to be polite about it.

"I've never seen anyone look at food like it was their lover before, but you're managing it."

I turned toward the feminine voice, swallowing the caviar as I spotted her.

She was pretty, with blond hair and sparkling brown

Midnight Moon

eyes. She was about my age and height, but she'd dressed in a men's tux with the black shirt collar undone.

I said the first thing that popped into my head. "I like your outfit."

She grinned. "Thanks." Her gaze moved to the food. "What's good?"

"All of it."

She laughed and picked up a plate, piling it high. "I hate gatherings like this. So stuffy and full of protocol. The only good part is the skiing."

"That bloodbath?" I took a glass of champagne from a passing waiter. Snagging one for her as well, I handed it to her, and she accepted It with a smile.

"Thanks." She tilted the glass toward mine, and we clinked. "Health and happiness."

"I like that toast." I sipped, the sparkling wine tasting like bright, pure heaven as it rolled over my tongue.

"The skiing is great," she said. "And you did super well for your first time."

"Thanks. I'm Lyra, by the way."

"Phoebe." She held out a hand, and we shook. "You're here with Garreth?"

I nodded. "You?"

"City Pack."

I felt my cheek twitch, and suddenly found myself questioning our easy camaraderie.

"Yeah." Her voice was low. "Sorry about that. I know

that the alpha is threatening your friend, and I don't agree with it."

"You know what he plans for Meg?" Fear iced my spine.

She nodded, her gaze shadowed. "He has two men watching her apartment, night and day. Plans to grab her if you need extra motivation."

The reminder of the threat made anger flash inside me. It had felt nearly impossible not to warn Meg, but Montblake had made it clear what would happen if I did. "Why are you telling me this? Are you threatening me, too?"

She shook her head, her gaze moving toward Garreth. "No. I... I feel guilty. I used to be in the Olympia Pack, before Garreth's father made it a horrible place to be. When the City Pack offered me a spot, I took it just to get away. I miss my family, though. And now this whole thing with you and your friend? It's gone too far. But the alpha won't back off."

"And no one will stand up to him?"

She shrugged, looking both angry and sad. "He's got an iron grip, even though I think our alpha is losing his marbles."

Shit. I didn't like the sound of that. "Do you think he'll deal honestly with Garreth?"

I already knew he wouldn't, but I wanted her take.

"I can't say, but..." She shook her head.

That was clear enough. "Thanks."

Midnight Moon

"Watch out for yourself," she said. "Garreth will protect the pack with everything he has. If he finds out you're betraying him...."

"I'm dead." I swallowed hard, fear twisting my insides.

She shrugged, worry on her face. "Maybe not. But... maybe. I know he's killed to protect the pack in the past."

I drew in an unsteady breath. "Thank you for the warning."

"Yeah. I need to go before my alpha notices me talking to you." She clinked her glass against mine one more time. "Nice to meet you, though."

"Thanks for the advice." I watched her walk off. This whole situation was a mess, and even though she was in Montblake's pack, I didn't think she was a bad person. In fact, she seemed trapped, too. Not in the same way I was, but she definitely wasn't happy about her situation.

I shook the thought away and took one last plate of food from the buffet, then turned to go mingle. As the evening wore on, I spoke to several different people. Even though they could turn into animals, they all seemed fairly normal.

Until I ran into Doreen.

She was an older woman, alpha of the San Andreas pack, and from the hard set of her jaw and the glint in her eyes, she took shit from no one.

As soon as I neared her, she barked, "What are you?"

I blinked, freezing. "Excuse me?"

"What are you? Species, girl, what species?"

"I, ah—" Instinct told me not to admit that I didn't know what I was. It was a weakness, and predators didn't respect weakness. This woman was most definitely a predator. I smiled, trying to look cunning. "I'm a Gemini. You?"

"You know that's not what I mean." She glowered.

A strong hand touched the small of my back, and I was suddenly wrapped in the scent of the forest. Relief rushed through me.

Garreth.

His gaze landed on the woman. "Doreen. Stop harassing my date."

"I just want to know what she is, that's all. I think we deserve to."

"No one here is entitled to anything." His voice was cold but his face polite.

Doreen growled at him.

"Enjoy your evening." He inclined his head toward her, then led me away.

I could feel her glowering at me as he murmured against my ear. "Avoid her."

A shiver rushed down my spine, and I barely managed to keep my voice steady as I said, "You'll hear no argument from me."

"I saw you speaking to Phoebe."

I nodded, debating what to tell him. A little bit of

Midnight Moon   137

honesty would go a long way here. He was so suspicious of the City Pack—and rightly so—that he wouldn't believe it if I had no interesting encounters with them.

"She doesn't seem to like their alpha much," I said.

"Really?"

I nodded. "Seems to miss her family back at your place, too."

"Not a surprise. Anything else?"

"It sounds like it was hard for her while your father was alpha. What was that about?"

"He...wasn't well."

I definitely wanted to dig more into that, but now wasn't the time. I could feel his gaze on me, waiting for more information. He suspected the City Pack already, so I wouldn't be revealing anything new with my next words. "I don't think she trusts Montblake to deal honestly with you. When I asked her, she wouldn't say it with words, but she shook her head."

"She wouldn't be able to speak against her alpha."

"I get the impression that Montblake keeps a tight leash on his pack members."

"Dictators often have to." Disgust sounded in his voice. "I can't believe I'm trying to come to an agreement with someone like him."

"You'd rather just duke it out, wouldn't you?" *If he's deceiving us, we'll kill him.* The words he'd spoken back at the Windracer came back to me. He'd probably been talking about Montblake.

He nodded, his fist flexing at his side. "Definitely." He sighed. "But I'll try diplomacy first. It's a new tactic for me, and best, considering two dozen of my former pack members are now in his clan. I want them back, but that can't be accomplished with brute force. Not without some of them getting hurt."

"Well, let me see if he approaches me," I said. "How much longer will this evening go?"

"Another hour or so. Maybe a bit more. I still need to speak to the alpha of the pack across the border."

"There are Canadian packs here?"

He nodded. "We aren't concerned with the borders established by humans." He stepped away. "I'll see you in a bit."

I watched him disappear through the crowd, then headed toward the side of the room. I'd stick to the shadows for now, and hopefully no one would see me.

Unfortunately, I wasn't so lucky.

Within ten minutes of finding a nice quiet spot behind a potted evergreen, Montblake found me. His eyes glinted with cunning as he took up a space in the shadows, and I realized that I didn't really need to tell Garreth that Montblake was dealing behind his back. The bastard would reveal that on his own.

He really was slightly off his rocker, like Phoebe had said. It was just a matter of time before he revealed his hand to Garreth.

"I have something for you," Montblake said.

Midnight Moon

"No thanks."

"You don't have a choice. Do you want me to tell Garreth that you're working behind his back?"

Shit.

Acid fear turned my stomach.

I'd had plenty of time to tell Garreth the truth and had chosen not to because it seemed too dangerous. But now my window of opportunity had closed. I was officially on Team Montblake now, and I knew what Garreth did to people who deceived him.

Had I handled this situation correctly, or bungled it until I was in a corner?

I ignored the tiny voice of doubt and focused on the problem at hand. I couldn't afford another enemy like Montblake. Especially not Garreth, who was much more dangerous. Not to mention, he currently held my job in his hands.

"What do you want?" I didn't care that my voice was cold.

He held up a tiny black pin, not much bigger than a pencil eraser. It looked like a little piece of jewelry. "I'd like you to wear this."

It would blend perfectly with my dress, being almost indistinguishable. "Why?"

"It's enchanted to provide a view of whatever you see. It will also transmit sound."

"You want me to wear a magical wire so you can spy on Garreth." Cold iced my spine. "No way."

"You don't have a choice. Unless you'd like him to know about you?"

Panic made my heart thunder.

Shit, shit, shit.

What should I do?

Take the thing for right now. Get him off my back. Then deal with it.

"Fine. Give me the damned thing."

He handed it over, and I pinned it to my dress, right near a seam where it would be less noticeable.

"I hate you," I said.

He just smiled. "Find the book."

The bastard disappeared before I could say anything, and I watched him go. Exhausted, I thunked my head back against the wall.

This was going to be harder than I'd thought.

I managed to avoid any more conversations for the rest of the evening. By the time Garreth found me to go back to the room, I was eager to get out of this snake pit.

Except for the fact that I wore a freaking magical wire.

"Are you ready to go?" he asked.

"More than."

As we walked down the hall toward our room, I chatted inanely. I didn't want to give Garreth an opportunity to say anything, lest it be overheard by Montblake. I might be betraying Garreth by trying to steal his book, but I could justify that because it would save my

Midnight Moon

friend. The book might be worth a lot of money, but not worth more than a life.

But this surveillance went a step too far. I couldn't do that to him.

And I *really* couldn't be caught wearing it.

Nor could I tell him about it because he might confront Montblake. Then Montblake would kill Meg.

How was I going to get rid of it, though? I couldn't keep talking about food for the rest of the weekend.

When I spotted a wrinkle in the rug up ahead, an idea flickered. I made sure to hit it as I walked, stumbling gracelessly to the ground. As I went down, I flicked off the tiny pin. It bounced along the floor and landed against the baseboards, hidden in shadows.

"Damned heels," I muttered. "Caught on the rug."

"Let me help you." Garreth gripped my arms and helped me gently to my feet.

As we walked away from the abandoned pin, relief rushed through me. At least we were alone, again. I didn't know if Montblake would buy that the disposal of the pin was an accident, but I hoped so. He wouldn't break into Garreth's room tonight, at least, and I still had time to try to wiggle out of this impossible scenario.

13

Garreth

I opened the door to our shared room and stepped inside, quickly scanning the interior for any kind of attack.

It was empty.

I inhaled, scenting the air.

No one had been here besides us.

Good.

I stepped far enough into the room to allow Lyra to enter, then turned to her. "You take the bed."

"I can take the couch."

"I insist."

"All right." She stood awkwardly by the door, and I realized what she wanted to ask.

Midnight Moon 143

"Do you need help with your dress?"

"Yeah." A faint pink flush rose on her cheeks. "Do you mind?"

"It's fine." Fine didn't even begin to cover it. I was desperate to get another glimpse of her skin, even though I knew it was a terrible, ridiculous idea.

It was just a thin strip of skin revealed by an open zipper. It shouldn't have such an effect on me.

And yet, I hadn't been able to stop thinking about it. Ever since I'd done up the zipper, I'd been thinking about undoing it.

She strode toward me, her glorious lavender and honey scent wrapping around me and squeezing tight. I'd had no idea I could be so attracted to someone.

But then, I'd never met my mate before.

She stopped in front of me and turned around. My head buzzed as I reached for her zipper. As I pinched the small tab, I heard her breath catch. Heat shot straight to my cock, and I gritted my teeth.

Not happening.

There was too much at stake, and I couldn't trust her.

"Did Montblake approach you tonight?" I asked, determined to move the moment away from attraction.

She let out a ragged breath. "He said hello. Asked how we met. He might have been fishing to see if he could recruit me, but he didn't go any farther."

I wasn't sure I believed her. There was something off

about her—she was jittery with nerves at the very least. Possibly a liar.

Untrustworthy.

I clung to that as I pulled the zipper down, revealing the pale skin of her back.

But I still wanted her. Still liked her, for fate's sake. It was ridiculous.

"Thanks." She darted away, hurrying toward the bathroom. "Just going to get changed."

I watched the door shut behind her, then let out a shuddering breath and dragged a hand through my hair. How was I going to survive the night?

One foot in front of the other.

The mantra had served me well when I'd been in the military on difficult assignments, and it would serve me well here, too. Quickly as I could, I found a pair of thin sweats and a t-shirt. Normally I slept naked, but that wasn't an option.

I stripped out of my suit and put on the sleepwear, pulling the shirt down over my head just as Lyra returned to the room. She wore an old pair of shorts and a ratty t-shirt with a summer camp logo.

The clothes had to be hers. It gave me an insight into her life. Just a tiny one, but I clung to it.

Her eyes moved to me, but her expression was unreadable. "You sure about the couch?"

I nodded, then threw myself onto it. The thing was just barely long enough, and I focused on trying to get

Midnight Moon

comfortable as I listened to her climb into the bed. I stared at the ceiling like it held the meaning of life. The last thing I needed to do was watch her climb into bed. The vision would haunt me.

The light flicked off, plunging the room into total blackness. It was a large space normally, but it shrunk to the size of a closet as soon as it became dark. My damned shifter hearing picked up every little rustle of the sheets and shudder of her breath.

It was an unbearable silence, fraught with visions of joining her in bed. Every inch of my body felt electric, and it was all I could do to stay on the couch.

So, I started talking. Anything to distract myself.

"How is it that you never knew you were magical?" I asked into the dark. "Did you not know your parents?"

She hesitated, and I held my breath. I wanted this answer. I wanted all her answers. Knowing more about her had suddenly become imperative, and not because I was looking for a distraction.

Because I wanted to know her.

I hadn't wanted to know a woman so badly in all my life.

Damned mate bond.

Finally, she answered. "I knew them both. But I had no idea they were magical. Had to be my father, though."

"How do you know?"

She hesitated again, but only briefly. "Because it

certainly wasn't my mother. She died of a drug problem when I was fourteen."

"I'm sorry."

"Me too."

"People in the magical world have drug problems, too, though."

"I just know she wasn't, okay?"

I didn't push any farther. Apparently, this was a sore subject. As the thought hit me, I realized that I'd done what the witch had told me to. I'd gotten Lyra to lower her guard by confessing to something personal.

I could use the spell to make her forget me.

But I wasn't ready.

You'll never be ready.

I ignored the voice and focused on Lyra. I could erase her memory later. For now, I needed her help.

I knew it was mostly an excuse. I wanted to keep her in my life, no matter how stupid and dangerous that was. Hell, there was every chance she was working with the City Pack.

I shook the thoughts away as she asked, "What about your father? He was alpha, but it was problematic."

"Yes. That's what I'm trying to fix." My tone shut down the conversation, which wasn't fair. She'd told me something about herself, and if I didn't reciprocate, she'd clam up. "My mother was human, though. It's why I joined the military."

Midnight Moon 147

"It's unusual for supernaturals to join the military?"

I nodded. "We mix with humans, but we don't generally live with them. My father fell for my mother, even though she wasn't his mate."

"Mate?" Curiosity echoed in her voice, and I cursed myself. She'd learn about fated mates eventually, but I didn't need her asking questions right now.

"Yes." I could hear the reluctance in my voice and tried to banish it. "Shifters have fated mates—a person that fate believes is perfect for us."

"So, love at first sight?"

"No. It's often hate at first sight, interestingly enough. But you feel more around your mate. Trust and desire and things you can't fight. With time, people often come to agree with fate." Not that I would ever be able to, even though I was starting to think that fate might know what it was doing in that regard.

Except for the fact that she was probably a liar.

"How long have you worked at the hotel?" I asked, wanting to change the subject.

"About four or five years, but I was just accepted to business school."

"And you want to go."

"Yes." Uncertainty echoed in her voice.

"You don't sound so sure."

She sighed. "I *was* sure, until this. It seemed like the best way to raise myself out of my shitty circumstances, but now that I know I'm a supernatural, I'm not even sure I can go back to the real world."

"You can, but it won't feel the same."

"I had a feeling you'd say that. But how do I figure out what I am?"

Guilt struck me. Did I owe it to her to help her?

It felt like I did. I couldn't just leave her out in the world, newly realizing she was a supernatural, but alone.

"It's not easy to find out what you are if you don't know by adulthood. But I could...help you." I couldn't believe I'd said the words. This was supposed to be a quick arrangement.

"Why do you care?" Confusion sounded in her voice, along with mistrust.

The truth spilled out of me, shocking in its candor. "I like you."

I could feel how stunned she was. I hadn't meant it in a weak, watered down way. No—there was a connection between us, soul deep. It was impossible for me not to feel it.

And it was the most dangerous thing I could do.

"But I don't want to like you," I said. "And now it's time to go to bed."

Lyra

Midnight Moon

. . .

But I don't want to like you.

Garreth's words echoed in my head the next morning. It had been a long night, and I'd barely slept during most of it. I'd been too aware of Garreth on the couch nearby. Too aware of the answers I'd given him.

Had we really shared all of that about ourselves? I'd never told anyone about my mother. And yet, when he'd asked, I'd found the words spilling out of my mouth. It had felt good to let go of that load—to share it with someone else.

And he'd said he liked me.

But I was afraid he'd kill me if he found out what I was really doing here.

How the hell had my life gotten so weird?

One day, I was just a girl, hiding out from the mob.

The next, I was magical and surrounded by werewolves.

And still trying to avoid the mob.

Not that they were really the mob. They were something worse.

I shivered and looked over at the bathroom door. The shower had just turned off, and Garreth would be coming out soon.

Please be wearing a shirt.

After last night, I couldn't bear to see him half naked. He was too attractive for my sanity. Not just how he looked—but his aura. It drew me to him, the strongest attraction I'd ever felt. It was almost unnatural it was so powerful, especially since I was downright scared of him.

Fated mates.

I played the word over in my mind. Were we...?

No. No way. That was crazy.

And yet, it would explain my crazy attraction despite the risk.

The door opened, and Garreth stepped out, fully dressed in jeans that loosely hugged his powerful thighs, and a green plaid flannel that made him look like the sexiest lumberjack I'd ever seen.

I sat upright, blinking. "You don't normally dress like that."

"I do, actually. The suits are my human disguise." He walked across the room with the grace of a large predator.

Hell, he *was* a large predator. A good-looking one.

At the door, he turned back with a thoughtful frown. "You haven't seen me enough to know how I normally dress."

"You're a guest at the hotel fairly frequently."

His eyebrows rose. "And you've noticed me?"

"Everyone notices you." Still, I flushed. "You're Garreth Locke, the most powerful man in the city. Why do you go to the city so much, by the way?"

"Business."

Midnight Moon 151

"Shifters have business with humans?"

"This shifter does. I've been working to repair our fortunes, usually through deals with human companies." He nodded toward the door. "I need to attend the last meeting today. This is where I'll either make headway with the City Pack or I won't. Take the time to do whatever you want. We'll meet for a last lunch as a group, and you can see if the City Pack approaches you."

"Sure." Guilt tugged at me as I watched him go.

Had he looked suspicious when he'd mentioned the City Pack? Did he know they had already contacted me?

No. He wouldn't let me in his room otherwise.

Speaking of...

I needed to use this time to look for the book. I doubted it was here, but I couldn't miss the opportunity.

Quickly, I scrambled out of bed and began to search the room. I was halfway done when a knock sounded at the door. I jerked upright from where I was looking under the mattress and hurried to the door, my heart pounding. When I opened it, I found a tall man carrying a tray full of food.

"Breakfast." He nodded into the room. "May I come in?"

"Sure. But I didn't order anything."

"The Olympia alpha had it sent up."

Garreth. Of course.

The man set the tray on the table and disappeared before I could figure out if I was supposed to tip. My stomach growled. The food smelled divine—bacon and eggs, with a side of thick, fluffy pancakes. A glass of orange juice sat next to a carafe of coffee.

As I sat to eat, guilt twisted in my stomach. Was I really going to steal something so valuable from Garreth?

It was just a book. Valuable, true. But just a thing. If I didn't, Meg would die. She was worth more than any book.

Angrily, I shoved pancakes into my mouth. They made me feel a bit better, and as soon as I was done, I kept searching for the damned book. What I really wanted to do was light the thing on fire. Make it so it was no longer a problem.

That fantasy wasn't going to come true today, however. I was nearly done searching when there was another knock on the door.

Lunch?

But no, it wasn't time. And we were supposed to meet down in the main room for a final lunch.

I opened the door and found Sam Montblake. I flinched. I hadn't been expecting him.

"Aren't you supposed to be meeting with Garreth?"

He grunted. "Done with that. He'll be here soon."

"Then you should go."

"I have a minute." His menace turned even darker. "Have you found the book?"

"I don't think he brought it, just like you said. Sorry."

Midnight Moon 153

"Sorry isn't good enough." His eyes iced over. "You need a bit of motivation, it seems."

Oh, shit.

I'd played my hand wrong—I could see it immediately. "Um, no. I—"

"I think you do. And I want to make sure you finish the job." He pulled a phone from his pocket, and a few seconds later, he spoke into it. "You can get her now."

No, no, no. "Please, no. Don't. I'll get you the book."

Panic flashed. I knew what was coming. He'd used the same damned phone to prove they were watching her.

He smiled coldly. "It will only take a moment. I thought we might be able to do this with just a distant threat, but it seems I was being optimistic."

I was babbling desperately but couldn't help myself. "I'll look harder, I promise. I will get you that book. You can count on me."

"Now I can." He turned the phone to me. "Because you have proper motivation."

Horrified, I watched the phone screen. It was in the middle of a video call, and the camera was aimed right at Meg's face. Her eyes were wide with fear, and the sight made my stomach turn.

"Meg! Meg, can you hear me?"

"Lyra?"

Montblake snatched the phone away so that I could no longer see her. "You have two days. And don't even think of telling Garreth what's going on, or I'll kill her before you can blink."

"I'll get it." I hated how my voice shook. Damn it, I was tougher than this. "And I won't tell him. Now get out of here before Garreth shows up."

"What about the pin I—"

I slammed the door in his face before he could finish the sentence, then leaned against it. He pounded on the door, but I ignored him.

Frantically, I texted Meg, hoping she would answer. Maybe the video had been some kind of impressive CGI.

Of course, it wasn't, and she didn't pick up.

My throat tightened as tears rose. She was in danger, being traumatized, because of me.

What the hell was I going to do?

14

Lyra

Garreth returned to the room, and I could barely meet his gaze. Fortunately, we went to the final lunch almost immediately. I didn't enjoy the activities with the were-wolves--it was all still way too unsettling—but I was grateful for the distraction. I made it through the event on autopilot, my gaze constantly scanning for Sam Montblake. He'd just been to my room to threaten me, but I wouldn't put it past him to bother me again.

He never approached me, thank God, and neither did any of the other City Pack members.

As we left, I caught sight of the woman I'd met at the previous dinner. She nodded at me, her gaze flicking toward Garreth, who walked by my side. There was a faint wistfulness there. Not romantic, but as if one were looking at an old family photo.

"I think she misses the pack," I murmured.

"What?" Garreth looked down at me, brow creased. We'd just reached his car, and he was about to open the door for me.

I nodded toward the woman, twenty feet away on the other side of the drive. "Your old pack mate."

She looked away before Garreth caught her gaze, but he frowned. "Let's go."

He opened the door for me, and I climbed in. We departed the lodge in silence. Garreth drove down the tree-lined road as fat flakes of snow began to fall.

Finally, I couldn't bear the silence any longer. "Were you successful?"

"Negotiating with the City Pack?"

"Yes."

He shrugged. "It seems that way."

"But you're doubtful."

"They have a history of being lying bastards. It's hard to trust someone like that."

Someone like me. I was intimately aware of the fact that I was lying to him, and I didn't like it.

"They didn't try anything else suspicious the entire time?" he asked.

I could hear the doubt in his voice and didn't blame him. He was no dummy. I wanted to stay by his side. Not just because I needed to get that damned book, but because I liked being with him. Which was insane, considering the danger I was in.

I was officially losing my mind.

I settled on a partial truth. "Sam Montblake did come to the room while you were gone today."

He glanced over at me in surprise. "Really?"

I nodded. "He said he was looking for you, but I had a feeling he was testing me out again. He asked for more details about our relationship. I think he might have been trying to see if I would be open to telling him more about you."

"And did you make it seem that way?"

"I tried to leave it open ended." Was he believing this? Could he see the guilt that twisted my insides?

"So, he's not dealing honestly with me," he said.

Relief rushed through me. Good. I was making sure he got the picture and knew the risk, but I wasn't outright betraying myself. Maybe I could walk this tightrope and get to the other side alive.

"What arrangement did you come to with him?" I asked.

"His pack is invited to our land on the next full moon. It's a coveted place to run."

"That's a big deal to shifters, isn't it?"

"Yes. Particularly to city shifters, who don't have the opportunity to take it for granted."

"When is the next full moon? Soon, right?"

He nodded. "In two nights."

My mind raced. I needed an invite back to his place if I wanted any chance at finding the damned book.

"I could come to your place and see if Montblake tries to fully recruit me," I said. "And you could maybe help me figure out what I am." I prayed he didn't hear the hope in my voice.

Garreth

Lyra's words echoed in my head. *You could maybe help me figure out what I am.*

The hope in her voice twisted my heart.

Of course, I had to help her.

Not because she was my mate, but because she was alone. A supernatural with no one. Helping her was the right thing to do. And I wanted to. The idea of being parted from her made my wolf grumble with distress.

She also seemed to be telling me the truth, at least about his visit to the room. I'd smelled Montblake when I'd returned to the room and wondered if he'd knocked or just come by to listen at the door.

Now I had my answer.

I'd expected him to try to play dirty, but it was

Midnight Moon

annoying all the same. I didn't like this diplomacy thing any more than he did, but it was the right thing for both our packs.

So what was he up to? And how did he want Lyra to factor in?

I needed to keep her close to determine that. And I still hadn't learned why she was in my room at the hotel to begin with. She was harboring secrets, and I wanted to get to the bottom of them.

"I like that idea," I said. "I'd appreciate it if you'd come back to Olympia with me. For a short time."

"Could we run by Seattle real quick so I can pick up my bike?"

"Your bike?"

"My motorcycle. It feels weird to drive into an unknown place with you without having a way to leave when I want to. Unless I'm a prisoner?"

"Of course not. Just tell me your address."

"It's parked at the hotel."

I put the hotel address into the GPS. When we arrived, she directed me around back to the alley where she'd parked. I stopped the car at the mouth of the alley, spotting a bike not far away.

She climbed out of the car and pointed to a motor-cycle in the parking lot. "I'll follow you."

"All right." I watched her stride to the bike, then confidently swing her leg over and turn it on.

She rode slowly toward me, and I pulled away from the curb, making sure she could keep up. It felt like I checked on her every other second—half because I wanted to make sure I hadn't lost her, and half because I wanted to see her.

Would she like my home?

I hoped so. It was stupid to want that, especially since I wasn't sure if I could trust her, but I couldn't fight it. I shouldn't care about her like this. I was going to erase her memory of me, after all.

But first, I'd help her figure out what she was. Once she had her footing in the magical world, I'd remove myself from her head and send her on her way.

It was nearly midnight by the time we turned onto the private road that would take us to Olympia. The moon was high in the sky and nearly full, illuminating the forest around us.

I tried to see it through her eyes—the enormous trees and the sparkling water up ahead. The huge house sat at the edge of the sound, the windows glittering brightly.

The road led right up to the house, circling around a huge oak tree in front of the main door. I parked in front of it, and she parked behind me. As I killed the engine, she climbed off her bike. I joined her at the base of the steps.

"You *live* here?" Awe sounded in her voice.

Midnight Moon 161

"With my pack. About fifteen people live in the house."

"How many bedrooms?"

"Thirty. It's been in the pack for generations."

"It's gorgeous."

"Thank you." *Thank you?* As if we were just doing a regular old house tour, when the reality was that I might be going crazy.

I'd just brought my mate to the pack. Even if I didn't say what she was to me, some pack members would sense it.

Shit.

I dragged a hand through my hair. Maybe this had been a bad idea. I'd been so pleased at the idea of having her with me that I'd invited her without really thinking.

But it was the smartest thing to do. And I owed her. I'd speak to the pack about keeping it quiet.

"You all right?" she asked.

I realized I'd been silent far too long. "Yeah, 'course. Let's go in. When it's morning, you can move your bike around to the garage."

"All right."

I fetched our bags, then led her through the massive wooden door inset with geometric panes of glass.

The scent of wood and water rushed over me as I walked into the massive main foyer.

Home.

The room stretched all the way to the back of the house, which was made primarily of glass. In the daylight, the multitude of windows would provide a phenomenal view of the sound. Right now, the gleaming glass reflected the large, modern furniture that filled the space.

A couple of the couches had pack members on them, reading or playing with their phones. It was late enough that most people were in bed, but the night owls waved briefly. I nodded at them, then turned to Lyra. Her eyes were wide as she took in the scene.

"This view must be phenomenal in the daylight. Like you're floating on the water."

I nodded. "It is."

"You're back!" A feminine voice sounded from the second story, and I looked up the wide floating staircase that led to the upper floors.

"Viv." I nodded to Lyra. "This is my...friend, Lyra." I barely hesitated before saying *friend*, but Viv caught it.

Her eyes widened as she looked at Lyra, and her lips parted on a silent gasp.

Shit.

She'd figured it out already.

It had taken Seth a few minutes, but Viv hadn't needed any time at all. Her gaze moved to me, and I shook my head subtly, trying to convey something along the lines of *keep your mouth shut.*

Her jaw tightened, and it was clear she got the

Midnight Moon   163

message. She looked back at Lyra and smiled. "Nice to meet you."

"Same," Lyra said.

"Can you get her a bedroom?" I asked Viv. "I've got a few things to see to."

"Sure thing, boss." She reached for Lyra's bag and took it. "Come on, I'll show you around."

"Thanks." Lyra gave me one last look, and there was the tiniest bit of uncertainty in it.

"I'll see you in a bit," I said, feeling stupidly guilty for leaving her. She'd be fine with Viv.

True, I was dropping her off in a house full of werewolves, which she'd had no idea existed twenty-four hours ago, but she'd proven herself tough.

She turned away and followed Viv up the stairs.

While they got settled, I went to find Seth. It didn't take long to update him on the final meeting with Montblake, but by the time I returned to the main room it was empty. The rest of the pack had gone to sleep, and I really needed to check on Lyra.

I met Viv on the stairs.

"Did you get her settled in the green room?" It was the room most commonly used for guests.

"Green room?" Viv's brows rose. "I put her in the blue room."

I felt my jaw slacken. "The blue room? Really?"

She grinned, and there was a mischievous glint to her eye that made me growl low in my throat.

"What?" she said. "She's your mate. Of course, she needs the room that adjoins yours."

"I don't know what you think you're trying—"

"Of course, you do. I like her, and I think she'd be good for you."

"You know I can't have a mate."

"Well, you do. And you'd be stupid to ignore her." Viv's eyes widened. "Hang on a sec. Doesn't she *know* she's your mate?"

"No. And I assume you didn't mention it?"

"Of course not." She laughed. "I can't believe this."

"You're going to have to. Because we're going to help her find out what she is, and then send her on her way."

"You need her, Garreth. I've known you for years, and you *need* her."

"I'm fine."

She scoffed, clearly disgusted.

"You know what happened to my father. So, drop it."

"You're a different person."

"Which is why I'm going to have the self-control to put my pack first. Goodnight, Viv."

She sighed and stepped aside so I could pass. As I climbed the stairs, I cursed her meddling. The room next to mine was a relic of the past. It had been intended to be a sitting room, but one of the previous alphas had refurbished it as a bedroom. It had never changed, but we didn't generally put guests in it.

Of course, Viv had.

Midnight Moon

I should've known. She was a meddler by nature and soft hearted.

Too late to move Lyra now. It would make a bigger scene, and it wasn't like I needed to open the door between our rooms.

Even so, my heart beat faster as I approached the side-by-side doors.

15

Lyra

Holy shit, how was this my life?

I stood at the massive wall of glass, staring out at the bright moon. Its light glittered on the water, and I couldn't believe the beauty of the view.

Or the room.

It was a modern masterpiece, all simple lines and gleaming wood. More beautiful than any room I'd ever been in.

And Viv had been so nice. She'd chatted all the way up the stairs and the whole time she was getting me settled. A magnificent meal had been delivered, and we'd eaten steak and buttery mashed potatoes together, downing a bottle of red wine in the process.

Midnight Moon 167

The whole evening had been amazing, and I'd been surprised at how well we'd gotten along. Friendship had never been so easy with anyone. Even with Meg, whom I loved more than anyone, it had taken a long time.

But with Viv, we'd just clicked.

Was it because I was a shifter like her?

God, I hoped I found out what I was. Soon.

I hated not knowing, almost as much as I hated the sticky spot I was currently in. If only my life had been normal...

But no.

I shook my head.

A normal life had never been for me, and I didn't even really want one. This had just turned out to be even crazier than I'd expected.

When a knock sounded at the door, I whirled around.

Viv?

No. As I approached it, I knew who it would be.

Garreth.

I sensed him, as if the air were suddenly alive with an electric current generated by his magnetism.

My heart thundered as I swung open the door and looked up at him. As usual, he towered over me, his broad shoulders filling the doorway. His beautiful face was set in too-serious lines, and I realized that I very rarely saw him smile. The weight of everything that rested on his shoulders clearly took a toll on him.

And yet, he was still helping me, inviting me here to figure out what I was.

Gratitude filled me, and I threw my arms around him in a hug.

He stiffened in shock, and so did I.

Holy shit, what was I doing?

I wasn't a hugger. And Garreth *definitely* wasn't.

Not to mention, I was in a seriously dangerous situation with him, and I didn't trust him.

But here I was, hugging him because I was happy and grateful.

"Thanks for everything," I muttered against his chest, somehow unable to unlock my arms from around his back. I was frozen in a weird stasis, locked in position by desire and awkwardness in equal portions.

Slowly, his arms closed around me, enveloping me in warmth and the scent of the forest.

Even though I'd intended to pull back, I sank deeper into the embrace, breathing in his scent. I couldn't tell if I wanted to kiss him or just snuggle into him for sixty hours straight.

I'd never felt so protected in my life. It wasn't a logical thing. My logical mind knew he was a threat to me. But deep in my gut, I felt the warmth of comfort and protection.

I *knew* I couldn't trust him, and yet I still liked him. Still wanted him.

It was a real mind fuck.

Mates.

He had mentioned fated mates. Could that be why I felt this way?

No, that's crazy.

His arms tightened around me in one quick embrace, then he stepped back.

I flushed, my cheeks hot, and barely managed to meet his gaze. "It's just, ah, that I really appreciate your help."

He nodded. "Of course. Get some sleep, and tomorrow we'll go to the witch who lives on the property. She can help figure out what you are."

"Thanks." I smiled, still feeling a bit awkward as my heart raced. His gaze lingered on me for the briefest moment, and I wondered what it would be like to kiss him.

Amazing.

Instead, he turned and walked away.

I shut the door, then leaned against it.

"What the hell am I doing?" I squeezed my eyes shut. I was here to steal from him—something really valuable —and he was going to hate me. I'd also spent the last couple days fearing for my life, though I was having a harder and harder time believing he would actually kill me.

I shook away the thoughts and climbed into bed. I had to do this for Meg, and until I'd saved her, I couldn't be wasting time worrying about Garreth.

The next morning, I moved my bike in the garage, then enjoyed a heavenly shower in the giant bathroom. I'd just finished dressing when I heard the knock.

I opened the door, and Viv grinned widely. "Morning! Ready for breakfast?"

"Um, sure." I grinned, and my stomach growled. "Really ready, apparently."

"Me too. I freaking love breakfast. And George makes the best."

"George?"

"The cook." She grabbed my hand and pulled me out into the hall. "Come on, let's go before the good seats are taken."

I smiled, laughing as she pulled me down the hall.

Was this really my life?

How was I having so much fun, and all before nine am?

Guilt struck me. Meg was currently captive. I shouldn't be having fun when she was terrified.

Viv led me through the massive house, which was an art piece in and of itself. The halls were wide, the floors made of huge, gleaming planks of wood. There was glass everywhere, providing a phenomenal view of the water and forests surrounding us. A narrow river flowed down the right side of the hallway, glittering water rushing over gray pebbles.

Midnight Moon   171

"There's a *river* going through your house?" I asked.

"Man made."

"Duh. But it's...crazy."

"Nice, right? We've got the best land and house on the west coast. It's a great place to live."

Envy struck me. Not just for the beautiful house and surroundings, but because they lived here as a group. A family.

I hadn't had a family in so long I couldn't even remember what it was like.

She led me to a large, airy kitchen. Like the rest of the house, it had massive windows made of glass. Sunlight gleamed on the huge appliances and beautiful wooden cabinets. A long trestle table was filled with people—mostly women, but a couple men as well. They drank coffee and chatted, some playing on their phones and others reading a newspaper.

A man bustled around the kitchen, tossing eggs in a pan, and pulling bacon out of the oven.

"Hello, lovelies!" he called out. "Just in time for breakfast!"

"Thanks, George." Viv grinned, then pointed to me. "This is Lyra. She's visiting for a little while."

"Lyra, my love, do you drink coffee?"

"I do."

"Then help yourself to the pot over there." He used a spatula to point to a side table bedecked with coffee and pastries. My stomach growled at the sight of it, and he laughed.

The morning passed quickly as we ate and drank with the rest of the group. Garreth never showed up, and eventually I stopped looking at the door and paid attention to the people I was meeting.

They were all so nice that it was easy to forget they could turn into wolves, whenever they wanted.

When lunch was over, Viv gave me a tour of the grounds. Though I'd loved the house, nothing could compare with the land surrounding it. In full daylight, I could see the massive forest and the wide expanse of glittering water.

"It's a paradise," I said.

"You live in the city?"

"I do."

"Not easy for a shifter."

"Is that what you think I am?"

"Not sure, but if I had to bet, that's what I'd put money on."

"But I could be any animal, right?"

"Yep."

"Hedgehog, even?"

She scrunched up her face in a laugh. "Possible. Not probable, though. Shifters tend to be larger animals. Predators, most of the time."

I blew out a breath, unable to imagine what I might

turn into. When I was here, it was easy to forget the real world that haunted me.

As if my troubles knew that I was thinking about them, my phone buzzed. I pulled it out of my pocket to check and saw a text message. When I opened it, the photo on the inside chilled my soul.

Meg.

She looked more tired, and the sight twisted my heart. But the message was clear.

Do what we want, or we'll hurt her.

"Are you all right?"

Viv's voice snapped me out of my funk, and I looked up. Shit. I hadn't been breathing.

"I'm fine. Just a message saying I'm late on my rent." It was close to the truth—I was often late on my rent—and it was a good reason to look freaked out. Still, guilt tugged at me. I hated lying to her.

I shoved the phone back in my pocket and drew in a deep breath. "Is there a library here?"

"Sure. Do you like to read?"

"Love it." But that wasn't why I wanted to know. There was a chance that Garreth had put *the* book there.

"Come on, I'll show you."

Like the rest of the house, it was magnificent. Thousands of books covered the shelves, seemingly miles of them. The room had been built in a part of the house that had fewer windows, no doubt to protect the volumes from light, and it had a cozy feeling that made me want to curl up and read for days.

I shoved the thought aside and began to walk along the shelves, wondering how the hell I was *ever* going to find this thing.

"Are you looking for anything in particular?"

"Um... something about wolves, I think." I *was* genuinely interested in them, considering I was currently living amongst a whole lot of them. It was just a lucky coincidence that I'd seen the title of the book while snooping in Garreth's hotel room: *The History of the Wolves of North America.*

"Over here." Viv led me to the far corner of the room. She gestured to four huge bookcases, and my jaw dropped.

"That's a lot of wolf books."

"Well, we have a particular interest." She grinned.

"You're telling me."

Garreth

The meeting with my lead wolves passed in a blur. We were supposed to be talking about how it had gone with the City Pack—and we had—but my mind had been entirely on Lyra.

Midnight Moon 175

Was she doing all right? Was she frightened of the wolves?

Frightened probably wasn't the right word for a woman as tough as her. Very little scared her. Even when she'd seen the City Pack shift, she'd been more shocked than anything.

Finally, the meeting was over.

Viv had joined us halfway through, and I gestured to her as the others filed out of the room.

"How is Lyra settling in?"

"Seems to be taking it all in stride. I like her."

"Me too. I don't trust her, but I like her."

"Oh, I know." She gave a knowing smirk.

"Keep it to yourself."

She shrugged. "I just think you could use some company."

"Company? Is that what you're calling it?"

"I didn't think you'd appreciate me being more graphic." She grinned wider. "But I'm happy to if you want me to be."

"No, I'm good. Where is she now?"

"In the library, last I saw. Looking for books on wolves."

"She wants to know more about us."

"And herself."

I nodded. "I need to take her down to see Kate. Maybe the witch can help her figure out what she is."

"I can do it."

"No, I will." I wanted to spend time with her, even though I knew it was a dangerous idea. I found it difficult to be parted from her, and my life was full of difficult things. I didn't want to add another one to the mix.

"All right." She smiled, giving me a knowing look that I ignored.

I parted ways with Viv and found Lyra in the library. She was curled up in a chair, immersed in a book as the golden lamps cast an ethereal glow on her face. She looked like she belonged, and my heart thudded at the sight of her.

I could still feel the hug she'd given me last night, as if her arms had imprinted on me. I wanted to feel it again. To feel more.

Was I really going to erase her memory?

Yes. I had to. I was still cleaning up the mess my father had made. I couldn't do the same thing he had. I still didn't know if I could trust her, and even if I could, I couldn't afford a distraction.

"Lyra."

Her head snapped up, and her eyes widened. "Garreth. What are you doing here?"

"I wanted to know if you'd like to go visit our resident witch. She might be able to help you figure out what you are."

She shut the book gently and hopped up, her eyes bright. "Definitely. Let's go."

I waited while she stashed the book on the shelf,

Midnight Moon 177

making a note of which one it was. I wanted to know more about her, and the books she liked were a good place to start.

"You like to read?" I asked as I led her down the hall.

"Love it. I feel like Belle from *Beauty and the Beast* in a library like this."

"That makes me the Beast."

She shrugged. "You said it, not me."

"Is that really how you see me?" Was that the slightest note of hurt that I heard in my voice?

How humiliating.

She looked up at me, eyes calm and intent. "I don't know. I've never seen you turn into a wolf."

"You'd like that?" Something warmed inside me at the idea, and my wolf rumbled his pleasure.

"I won't know until I see it."

"Maybe later." It was a terrible idea, of course. Anything that would bond us was a terrible idea.

Fortunately, we had reached the front door, and it was such a beautiful day that it distracted her from the conversation.

"I can't believe this weather." She spun in a circle in the drive, her arms outflung and her long hair spinning around her. "It's the middle of winter, and this sun is glorious."

She looked so beautiful in the sunlight that it took my breath away. I couldn't even form words to create a response, and when she looked at me, it was all I could do to nod.

"Which way to the witch?" she asked.

"Down to the water." I nodded toward the pier that stretched into the sound. Kate's boat bobbed at the end, and I could see her on the deck, staining the wooden trim.

Lyra and I walked in silence down to the boat, and I forced myself to keep my attention on the water ahead. I wanted to stare at Lyra for hours, which was both ridiculous and dangerous.

As we stepped onto the dock, Lyra said, "I've never been on a boat."

"No?" I realized I didn't know much about her.

"Nope. Not really part of my lifestyle."

It took physical effort to stop myself from asking more about her.

As we approached Kate, the witch stood and stuck her brush in the can of wood stain. She wore old jeans and a ragged sweatshirt, her red hair pulled up on her head.

"Bringing me a visitor, Garreth?" she called.

"Lyra is her name." I gestured to Kate. "Lyra, this is Kate. Our resident witch."

"Wow." Lyra grinned. "A real witch? With spells and everything?"

"Everything except the wart on the nose. That comes with time, like a badge of honor."

Midnight Moon 179

Lyra laughed.

"So, what brings you to my boat?"

"Lyra is a supernatural, but she grew up with humans. She doesn't know what she is."

"Ah. And you want my help." Kate tilted her head to study Lyra. "I can try, at least."

"Thank you. *So* much." Lyra grinned widely. "It's so strange to think I might have magic but not know what it is."

Kate saluted. "Well, I'm at your service. Come aboard."

Lyra stepped toward the boat, and I followed.

"Not you, pal." Kate waved me away. "This is girls' business. You head on up to the house again."

"All right." I gave Lyra and Kate one last look, curious what they would find out.

They both waved, but as I walked away, it was impossible not to look back at her one more time.

16

Lyra

"So, you're an unknown supernatural?" Kate looked me up and down again, her mouth pursed as if she were trying to solve a mystery.

"Yep. Can you really help me with that?"

"I can try. Let's visit my workshop." She led me across the deck and down into the cabin. It was a narrow, crowded space full of tiny bottles and a cauldron that sat in the boat's little kitchen.

"A bit cramped, I know. But it works for me."

"Do you have a coven?" Was being a witch like they showed on TV?

Her gaze went slightly dark, and she shook her head. "Not anymore."

Midnight Moon

It was obviously a sore subject for her, so I changed it. "All this stuff is amazing. Are these tiny bottles full of ingredients for you spells?"

"They are." She brightened. "Most of them I collect from the woods, but some of the rarer ingredients need to be bought from vendors."

"Vendors? Like in the city?"

"Yep. Their shops are hidden from humans using magic. We don't need people wandering in and seeing a vat of newts, now do we?"

"Do you really use newts?"

"Nah. But we use plenty of other weird stuff. Now sit down." She pointed to a bench along one wall. "I need to mix some stuff up."

I did as she commanded, watching while she gathered supplies and began to measure them into the cauldron.

"So, you and Garreth..." She let the sentence trail off.

"Yeah, I can feel everyone's curiosity, but there's nothing there."

"Ha. As if I'll ever believe that."

"I'll admit, there's some attraction, but that's it."

She shot me a strangely knowing look over her shoulder.

"What?"

"Nothing." She shrugged. "He seems tough, but he's not a bad guy. He's a bit hard after all his time in the military and the weight of his work here, but he's a good egg."

"A bit hard? I've heard stories that he's killed people who betrayed him."

"That's part of being alpha and protecting the pack."

I swallowed hard. *Protecting the pack.*

If he found out about my betrayal, would he think I was threatening the pack? Hopefully not. I was just stealing something valuable, that was all.

"His father really screwed up, huh?" I wanted more info about that.

"I wasn't here to see it, but yes." She hesitated, clearly not wanting to talk about the details. "Garreth gave me a place when my coven kicked me out. I'll always owe him for that."

"Oh, shit. I'm sorry. I don't understand how that works, but it sounds bad."

"It was. Anyway—" She scooped some of the liquid she'd brewed into a tiny cup. "Let's do this thing."

I nodded, staring at the cup. "What do I do, drink it?"

"Yep. And then I chant a spell. With any luck, we'll get an idea of what you are." She thrust the cup toward me.

My hand trembled slightly as I reached for it. I couldn't believe the turns my life had taken. Just the other day, I'd been cleaning the rooms at the Windracer. Now I was about to drink a witch's potion while on land owned by werewolves.

Midnight Moon 183

"Bottoms up," I said, then tossed it back.

The brew tasted both sweet and bitter, an odd combination. I swallowed quickly, then gasped. "Now what?"

"Just hang tight." She stood in front of me with a book in her hands and began to chant, occasionally consulting the pages for the next words. It was all in a language I couldn't identify, but I could feel the power spark on the air. It almost felt like there was an electric current flowing around us, prickly but not painful. As it increased, my body began to vibrate.

"This is crazy." I squeezed my eyes briefly, trying to get control of my body.

Kate finished chanting and said, "Open your eyes."

I did and gasped. A figure made of smoke stood next to her. It was definitely a four-legged animal, but it was impossible to tell what.

"You're big, whatever you are," Kate said.

"No kidding." The back of the smokey creature was nearly at her chest. It had slender legs and a powerful body, but the face lacked any detail. It could have been a giant cat or a werewolf or something I'd never heard of.

"It's the best I can do at the moment," Kate said. "You're definitely a shifter. If I can get some different ingredients, we might be able to pinpoint it better."

"So, I could be a wolf."

"Yep. Is that what you want?"

"I don't know." But I did know I'd like to belong to

this pack, whatever I was. I finally felt like I was at home, even though it was crazy to think that after such a short time.

Not that I'd ever be welcomed if I stole their book. And I couldn't live with myself if I let something happen to Meg.

As if she could read my mind, Kate said, "I get it."

"You miss your coven, don't you?"

She nodded. "But it is what it is."

She clearly wanted to move on from the subject, and I didn't mind. I was still so curious about what we'd found. "If I'm a shifter, why have I never shifted?"

"Only one of your parents was magical, right?"

"I think so. I didn't know them well." Even though I'd lived with my mother until she'd died when I was fourteen, she'd been an enigma. Distant and troubled.

"You probably need a catalyst. An intense event or something similar."

I blew out a breath. Hadn't I already had an intense event? When Sam Montblake had busted into my apartment and slammed me against the wall, that had definitely felt like an intense event. If only I'd been able to turn into a giant animal and attack him.

But then, he'd have turned into a damned mountain lion and attacked me back.

I stood. "Thanks for the help, Kate."

"Anytime. I'll see if I can get ahold of those ingredients that might give us a better idea of what you are."

"You're a lifesaver. Do you know where I might find Garreth?"

"This time of day? Probably his office. Second floor, east side of the house."

"Thanks." I hurried away, heading toward the house. The cool wind whipped my hair back from my face and brought with it the scent of the sea. I drew the air deeply into my lungs, feeling like my soul settled into its happy place when I was outdoors here. This place was so wonderful that I almost couldn't believe it was real.

It didn't take me long to find Garreth's office. It was exactly where Kate had said it would be, though it was nothing like I had imagined. Instead of a boring room full of papers and a computer, it was a palace of light and color. Two of the walls were made entirely of glass, giving the occupant the most incredible view of the sound and forest. The other walls were covered in massive paintings, modern masterpieces of color and shape. Tall bookcases stood between them, packed with books of all shapes and sizes.

The desk was a huge slab of wood, and there were comfy couches scattered around, along with coffee tables covered in more books. Garreth stood with his back to the door, gazing out at the view beyond.

I knocked on the open door. "Hi."

He turned, his face blank. There was the slightest twitch to his mouth, however, and it was hard not to think that it might be a smile.

"You like to read, too?" I asked, gesturing to all the books.

"I do."

I walked into the room and approached one of the shelves. What kind of books did he favor?

"Did you discover what kind of magical species you are?" he asked.

"A shifter. Big one. But not sure what." I ran my gaze over the shelf, looking for the book that the City Pack wanted. I wished I didn't have to do it.

When my gaze landed on it, my jaw nearly dropped.

I'd found it.

Quietly, Garreth approached. I heard him coming but didn't turn around. "Kate says she can maybe get a better idea of what I am with different ingredients. It will take a little time, though."

"Stay here in the meantime." His voice sounded close, and I could feel the heat of him against my back. It distracted from the book in front of me, and I inhaled as his scent wrapped around me, the most glorious forest aroma.

"Really?" I turned to look up at him. "One minute you're blackmailing me to help you at the winter gathering, and the next you're offering me a place to stay?"

"Sorry about the blackmail." His voice was rough, his pupils dilated. It was as if he, too, were affected by our nearness. It didn't matter that I didn't trust him, and

Midnight Moon 187

he probably didn't trust me. Desire was influencing our minds.

"I don't think I can take any more time off work," I said. "I'm supposed to start again tomorrow."

"I can make an arrangement with Boris."

I didn't like the sound of that—two powerful men discussing me and my fate and who would have my attention. True, Boris only wanted me to clean the rooms, and Garreth wanted me to...

What *did* he want from me?

At this point, I couldn't quite tell. "Are you helping me out of the goodness of your heart?"

"I don't know." His gaze moved over my face, and I swore that I could see heat ignite in his eyes. "I can't seem to help myself where you're concerned."

He stepped forward, close enough that his chest brushed against mine. The contact was enough to ignite a bomb between us. The tension exploded, and I gasped.

Garreth leaned down to kiss me, his mouth landing on mine with a ferocious grace that stole my breath and heated my blood. He tasted like heaven and kissed like the devil, and I shivered as his tongue slipped inside my mouth.

Unable to help myself, I wrapped my arms around his neck and pressed my body full against his. Suddenly, it became clear that *this* was the reason we'd been tiptoeing around each other. We'd both known that if we gave in to our desire, it would be an inferno.

A low growl of need sounded in his throat as he pulled me hard against him. His talented lips moved to my neck, lighting me up inside. I moaned and tilted my head to the side so that he could have better access. His tongue slid over my skin, and shivers raced over every inch of my body.

How could desire like this be real? I'd never felt anything so amazing in all my life.

Without warning, he pulled back. "I need to go."

I blinked. Before I could say anything, he'd spun away and left the room.

I stood there, shocked, for a half second.

What had just happened?

I had been stupid. Incredibly, ridiculously stupid.

A second later, Viv appeared.

"Knock, knock!" she called as she rapped on the door.

"Hi." I smiled, trying not to look like a lunatic. Was my face still flushed and my eyes glassy? My lips had to look swollen, too. I cringed slightly.

Viv didn't seem to notice. Or, if she did, she was good at hiding it. "Want to join me and the girls for dinner?"

"Um, sure. Who are the girls?"

"Just some other women in the pack. We eat together on Wednesday nights."

Midnight Moon

"Awesome. Thanks for inviting me."

"Come on." She led me down the hall toward the stairs. We climbed up the wide floating planks to the second level, and then to the third. From there, we went to the other side of the house. A huge glass door led to a top deck patio that gave a magnificent view of the water and mountains.

"Take this." She grabbed a big coat off the rack near the door and handed it to me.

I shrugged into its warmth, and she did the same with her coat. Together, we stepped out into the cool evening air. The temperature had dropped, but there were tall propane heaters scattered throughout the space, along with fire pits built into beautiful tables.

A group of women sat around one, drinking wine and chatting. There were four of them total, and when they spotted us, they waved.

Immediately, I felt welcomed.

How the hell were the shifters so good at that? They hardly even knew me and still, they welcomed me like I was one of their own.

As soon as I stole from Garreth, this would be over.

I shoved the thought aside.

Viv made the introductions and got me a glass of wine. I took a seat between two dark-haired women— Lora and Monica. The night passed in a blur of conversation and booze. It was a lovely time—something I'd never experienced before. This had to be what the other girls at the hotel did when they went out together.

Except here, I felt like I fit in.

As it got darker and darker and the night got colder, we turned up the lanterns and switched to hot chocolate. It tasted divine, and I couldn't help but look up at the stars and glorious moon above.

"It will be the full moon soon," Viv said.

"Do you guys change into wolves then?" I asked.

"We don't have to, but we like to." Viv gestured to the land around us. "We have hundreds of acres hidden from human eyes. Almost no pack has as much as we do. We like to take advantage of it and run 'til dawn."

It sounded amazing.

Strange, but amazing.

Finally, the night was over, and we turned off the lamps and cleaned up our mess. As I left the gathering, I realized that I didn't want to betray Garreth. What if the book was worth more than money, after all?

He was dangerous, but after that kiss, there was no way he would kill me.

Right?

He could even help me save Meg. Wouldn't I have a better chance with him by my side?

Just the thought of trusting him made me feel crazy. It went against everything I'd ever believed in my life.

Trust only yourself.

Midnight Moon 191

But I couldn't resist the siren song of coming clean. Maybe I could visit him and feel him out.

Decided, I hurried toward his office. Hopefully he would still be there, and my instinct would be correct. I barely knew him, but he seemed honorable.

As I reached his office, I heard the low sound of voices. Too quiet for most people to hear, but my ears could pick up anything.

The first thing I heard was my name. The second, the tone.

It wasn't good.

I tucked myself back against the wall and listened, my heart pounding.

"You're sure you want to use the potion on her?" Kate asked.

"She's not one of us. You know it's the wisest thing."

She's not one of us. Pain stabbed me.

"Erasing her memories is a big deal, though."

Erasing my *memories?*

Holy shit, he was going to erase my memories? Was that what this was all about?

Why?

He doesn't want you to know they exist.

If there was anything I'd learned here, it was that secrecy was everything to these wolves. And I knew something I shouldn't.

He hadn't invited me here to find out what I was.

He'd invited me here to keep an eye on me until he could erase my memories.

Bastard.

"You really think this is in the best interest of the pack?" Kate asked.

"I do. They agree."

They agree?

Did that include the women I'd met tonight? They were part of the pack, after all. And they had asked me a lot of questions about myself. I'd thought they were just interested and friendly, but when I thought back on the night....

When in my life had anyone been that interested in me?

Never.

Oh, my God, I was such a fool.

These people had tricked me all along.

Anger rose inside me, dark and thick.

My whole life, I'd been a pawn. First, played by my father. Then by my boss, and now by Garreth and his pack.

I was such an idiot.

Hot tears gathered in my eyes, but I blinked them back.

I knew I couldn't trust others, but for the briefest, most glorious time, I'd forgotten that. I'd lived like a normal person.

Stupid.

Midnight Moon

My father had proved to me years ago that you couldn't trust anyone, and now Garreth and his pack were confirming it.

I needed to get myself out of this horrible situation and move on.

I'd steal the book. It was the only way to save Meg.

17

Lyra

The next morning, I woke with a miserable headache and a hurting heart. I'd gone to bed last night without seeing Garreth. It hadn't been hard to sneak away from his office without him noticing. He was too busy plotting my downfall with Kate.

Could I even trust what she'd told me about myself? She was clearly colluding with him.

Everyone here was colluding.

What a nightmare.

I squeezed my eyes shut briefly, sucked in a deep breath, then rose. By the time I showered and dressed, it was midmorning. There was a knock on my door as I

Midnight Moon

was heading toward it, and I opened it to find Viv standing on the other side.

She grinned widely when she saw me, and for the briefest moment, I believed it.

Then I remembered yesterday.

"Hi." I tried to keep my voice from showing the hurt I felt. "What's up?"

"Tonight is the full moon. I thought you'd like a tour of the grounds before everyone gets here."

"Who is everyone?"

A loud roar caught my attention, and I turned to look out the window just as a helicopter landed on the yard outside.

Before she could say anything, I spotted a familiar figure climb out of the chopper.

Sam Montblake.

"Shit." I muttered.

"You know them?" Viv asked.

"The City Pack? Yes. I met them at the winter gathering with Garreth. That Montblake guy is creepy." Creepy was an understatement, but I didn't want to give anything away.

"Agreed. He's loaded, though. They've got a helicopter and everything. Which apparently allowed them to get here early."

Freaking perfect. Just what I needed.

"Do you want that tour?" Viv asked.

"Sure." I didn't know what else to do, and maybe it

would help me avoid Montblake. The last thing I wanted was to run into him. "Let's go."

The tour started on the grounds closest to the house, where there were several gardens planted. We walked along the beach and through the woods. The entire place was a natural wonderland, and a tiny bit of envy streaked through me. I hated feeling it, but it was hard not to contrast this with my everyday life in the city.

As we returned to the house, I spotted Garreth and Montblake standing on the main lawn.

"Let's skirt around them," Viv said. "Looks like they're talking about something important."

We made a wide loop around the lawn, but I couldn't take my gaze off the two alphas. Both men turned to look at me, and Garreth's gaze was colder than I'd ever seen it. I waited for it to warm upon recognizing me, but it didn't.

A shiver raced through me.

He really didn't care for me a bit, did he? I was just a pawn in this whole thing. He'd used me at the gathering, and now he'd brought me here so he could give me the potion that would make me lose my memory.

He wouldn't get the chance.

I looked away from him and hurried to the house behind Viv.

Garreth

I watched Lyra follow Viv into the house, careful to keep my gaze impassive. I didn't want Montblake realizing that I cared for her. He made my skin crawl, and the last thing I wanted was for his attention to turn toward Lyra.

"She's an interesting girl," he said.

"Hmm." I made sure there was disinterest in my tone, but I didn't like hearing him talk about her. "When will the rest of your pack arrive?"

"Right before dinner."

I nodded, wishing this damned event over and done with. That was a long way off, however. We needed to host a cookout first, then both packs would spend several hours roaming the grounds while in animal form. Hopefully, everything would go well, and we wouldn't have any vicious fights, but I wasn't holding my breath.

It was good to see old pack mates back on our land, however. Only two of them had come with Montblake, but more would be here later tonight.

Montblake nodded toward Kate's boat, which bobbed peacefully at its dock. "You really don't mind a witch living on your land?"

"Kate? No. She's helpful." She also thought that Lyra was strong enough to handle the truth of what she was to me. That she deserved to know.

It didn't matter. It was just too dangerous. After the kiss we'd shared, I knew I was starting to fall for her. I couldn't help it. If she stayed, I would be utterly under her spell.

Just like my father had been under his mate's spell. At that point, I'd become useless as alpha and Montblake would be able to complete his mission to take down my pack.

Was I really doing the right thing, trying diplomacy with him?

Odds on being able to trust him were so slim they were almost ridiculous.

But I had to try. Just the sight of my old pack members here, reunited with their family, was enough to motivate me.

I'd send Lyra back to her real life, none the wiser to my existence, but I'd still keep an eye on her from a distance. I would have to. I couldn't bear the thought of her out there in the world, alone and unprotected.

Montblake and I continued negotiations on which parts of the property his pack could run on and when, but my attention was partially on the land around me, hoping I would see Lyra again.

By the time our meeting was over, it was nearly time for dinner. More shifters from the City Pack had arrived, their vehicles pulling up the drive slowly, as if they were wary of an attack.

My pack mates had been setting up the barbecue

Midnight Moon   199

and tables for the last hour, lighting small fires in the portable fire pits and turning on heat lamps. Twinkling lights were strung amongst the trees surrounding the patio where we'd eat, and I couldn't remember ever seeing the place looking quite so good.

"Nice spread," Montblake said.

All I could hear was *And I'm going to take it from you.*

I nodded, watching him out of the corner of my eye.

When I spotted Lyra step out of the house, she distracted me from my wary guard. I looked toward her, my heart catching in my throat at the sight of her. She wore tight black pants that looked like leather, along with a large knit sweater that drooped off one pale shoulder. Her dark hair was swept over her shoulder and her lips were painted a bold, brilliant red.

Montblake whistled low under his breath, and I wanted to beat the hell out of him for it. Instead, I gestured toward the bar that had been set up near the stairs. "Why don't you get yourself a drink."

"Don't mind if I do." He ambled off to the bar, and I hoped he'd get so drunk we could just toss him in the sound.

No. That was poor diplomacy.

I turned from him, wanting a moment where I didn't have to think of the compromises I was making and wondering whether I was doing the right thing.

I walked up to Lyra, who drew me like a siren song. Could she tell that she was my mate?

How could she not feel the pull between us?

That kiss....

She definitely felt the pull. But she might not be able to identify what it was. Which was a good thing.

As I approached her, she watched me with dark eyes that looked like bottomless pools. Whatever she was feeling, I couldn't tell. But I desperately wanted to know.

I stopped in front of her, unable to resist drawing in a large breath of her scent. "Did you have a good day?"

The question was inane, but I found that I really wanted to know.

"Yes. It was fine." She looked around at the party that was starting to ramp up. People milled about, holding beers and glasses of wine while they congregated beneath the heat lamps and by the fire pits. The smell of roasting meat wafted from the large barbecues by the lawn, and music pumped through the air. "It was nice to see the land. It's gorgeous here."

"It really is. I couldn't love any place more." It was fate's honest truth. Nowhere compared to my home.

She looked toward the sky, where the full moon was beginning to appear. "You'll all turn into wolves and other creatures tonight?"

"We will. Does that worry you?"

She shook her head. "Humans are more dangerous than any wolf."

Did her gaze flick toward the bar?

Midnight Moon

I glanced over, spotting Montblake. He watched us with an impassive expression.

"He creeps me out," she said.

"I think he does that to everyone."

"I understand why you're alpha of the Olympia Pack, but why is he an alpha? He's not nearly as good a leader as you."

The words shouldn't have warmed my heart, but they did. "He's strong and ruthless. Sometimes, that's all it takes."

"Hmm. Well, I don't like it."

"Neither do I." But I'd be those things if I had to be. Erasing her memory would require it of me. "When dinner is over, stay in the house, all right? It might not be safe outside."

"You really don't trust them, do you?"

"I trust *my* wolves, but not the City Pack."

"Smart."

"Did Montblake say something to you?" Suspicion flickered through me.

"Nothing that I haven't told you. But he looks shady to me."

I couldn't blame her for thinking that. "I'll be leaving several of my pack here. They'll maintain human form and keep an eye on the house."

"Do they normally do that during a full moon run?"

I shook my head. "Just this time, while the City Pack is on our land."

She nodded. "Smart."

"They'll keep you company." *Keep you safe.*

It was more than half the reason I'd asked them to stay behind. She was too valuable to me, even if I did plan to erase her memory and send her away.

18

Lyra

Every second I spent talking to Garreth was torture.

How could he plan to erase my memory? I couldn't imagine anything crueler.

And yet, I still felt my heart twist whenever I thought of never seeing him again. It was insane.

When he left to make arrangements for the midnight run, I watched him go, unable to look away. This place was a fantasy kingdom, and he was its king. The crowd laughed and talked beneath the twinkling lights hanging from the trees. Fire pits crackled merrily as people roasted marshmallow's and drank mulled wine, and I could feel the heat of one of the lamps on my back.

Finally, the party lured me into its embrace. I couldn't spend the night staring at Garreth like an idiot. I needed to try to avoid Montblake. I couldn't believe he was here. I'd hoped I'd have more time—mostly so I could find another way around this miserable situation.

I dodged members of the City Pack as I made my way through the party, trying out the magnificent buffet but ignoring the open bar. As much as I might like a stiff drink right now, I needed to keep my wits about me. The food was an acceptable solace, however. The spread rivaled that at the winter gathering. The theme was more rustic—barbecue and picnic salads—but it was all ridiculously delicious.

Viv found me by the desserts, and we struck up a conversation, chatting as we ate double chocolate cake. It was far better than the free birthday cake that made up my normal indulgences, and I wasn't sure I could ever go back to that weak stuff.

"Come join us by the fire," Viv said.

"Sure."

"Awesome." Viv grinned, then pointed to a table on the other side of the patio. "That's us. I've got to run to the bathroom, but I'll meet you there."

"Okay."

She left, and I made my way toward the table full of women that I'd already met. I was halfway there when a voice called my name. "Lyra."

Seriously?

Midnight Moon 205

It was Montblake. I'd know his voice anywhere. It haunted my dreams, after all.

I tried to ignore him, pretending that I didn't hear as I cut through the tables and the crowd.

Unfortunately, he was fast. He caught up to me near the makeshift dance floor, his hand gripping my arm. I stopped, unable to get away without causing a scene.

"I thought that was you," he said, his voice falsely friendly. "We met at the winter gathering, didn't we?"

"Yes, I think so." I smiled, knowing it didn't reach my eyes. "Good to see you again."

"Likewise."

This charade was killing me.

It became worse when he lowered his voice. I could barely make out what he was saying, ensuring that no one else would be able to.

"You'll bring me the book tonight," he said.

"I don't know where it is."

"Liar."

Shit. "I really—"

"*Liar.* You know where it is, and you'll bring it to me at midnight."

"And if I don't?" I hissed, anger tightening my skin.

"I'll kill their alpha."

Horror shot through me, a fear so cold that it froze my bones. "You can't."

"Of course, I can."

"Then why didn't you do it sooner? If you could,

you'd have already done it. I see how much you hate him."

He smiled confidently and spread his arms wide. "I never had the access. Or the numbers."

Shit.

His voice was so cold, so determined, that I believed him.

I looked around, seeing the truth of his statement. There were more of the City Pack here. Garreth was clearly confident that his pack could hold them off, and I believed it. They had the advantage of being on their home turf, after all, and they might even be more powerful shifters.

But if Montblake went straight for Garreth, catching him by surprise with the backup he'd brought, he really could kill him.

Even though I didn't want to be afraid for Garreth, I was. I couldn't help it. Sam Montblake had been the bogeyman under my bed for my entire life. I hadn't known him, but he represented the people that my father had sold me out to.

"I see you're starting to understand," he said.

I swallowed hard and nodded. I'd always known I had to do this. They were too big a threat to Meg, after all. And now they'd added Garreth to the list.

"Fine," I whispered, my heart breaking. "Where do we meet?"

"There's a clearing in the woods. Follow the coast-

Midnight Moon

line to where the trees meet the water, then go inland. You'll find me there."

"All right."

He disappeared without another word, and I swallowed hard, a chill racing over my skin. This was going to be the most dangerous thing I'd ever attempted.

Was I really going to do this?

Yes.

I had to.

But I didn't have to do it yet. In fact, I couldn't. I'd need to wait until most people had shifted and left the party. So, until then, I would pretend for a little bit longer that I had a place here. Even if some of these people probably knew Garreth was trying to erase my memory, I could ignore that.

But it was hard. It was a constant reminder that I couldn't trust anyone. I found my spot at the table Viv had invited me to join, but everyone's friendliness twisted the knife in my heart. They chatted and laughed, trying to include me in the conversation. I hated it as much as I appreciated it.

For the second time, I realized that this whole thing was a real mind fuck.

Damn it, I wanted to get out of here and back to my normal, boring life.

"Are you all right?" Viv whispered.

"Yeah." I nodded, trying to look like everything was

ok. "Just a little too much food and drink, I think. I might go stretch my legs."

"Sure."

I stood, desperate to get away. The cold air at the edge of the party helped clear my head, but it didn't make me feel any less shit.

I tried to focus on the bright moon above and the strange sensation of it tugging on my soul. It calmed me a bit, and I let myself get pulled into its sway. But when I spotted Garreth on the other side of the party, my attention was helplessly riveted.

He was so powerful and graceful, yet there was something haunted about him.

His father? His past?

Why did I care?

Because I cared about *him.*

I shouldn't. It was stupid. Crazy, even.

And yet, I did.

I drew in a shuddery breath as I watched him walk through the crowd.

"You care for him." Kate's voice sounded from behind me, and I jumped.

When I turned, I spotted her leaning against one of the tables beneath a heat lamp, her arms crossed casually in front of her.

"I don't," I said.

"Liar."

I shrugged. "Doesn't matter."

Midnight Moon 209

"It does."

I looked at her, considering. From what I'd heard during the eavesdropped conversation, she disagreed with Garreth's plan. She could still be loyal to him, however. I decided to keep my mouth shut.

"Have you seen them shift before?" I asked.

She nodded. "All the time. But full moons are when everyone shifts and runs together."

Something in my soul called to the idea. Running amongst my fellow shifters—it sounded so crazy, but also divine.

But Garreth would never allow it. He wanted me gone so badly, he'd erase my memory.

"You know," Kate murmured, her eyes keen.

I raised my brows. "Know what?"

"His plans."

I tried for a confused expression. "What do you mean?"

"I wondered if I spotted you through the crack in the door last night, but until now, I wasn't sure if I did."

My heart began to thunder. I didn't want her to catch onto my plan.

"Don't bother denying it," she said. "I'm too clever."

I heaved a sigh and leaned against the table next to me. "What are you going to do about it, tell Garreth?"

"No. I don't agree with what he plans to do."

If I'd had any uncertainty about whether he was still planning to erase my memory, this just confirmed it.

I felt the pain of it like a spear through the heart.

"I shouldn't be so hurt by it," I said.

"Yes, you should. It's horrible."

"But you still made the potion for him."

"I made it before I met you, and it wasn't like I could fight him to keep him from taking it."

That was true. "And you're not going to tell him I know?"

She shook her head. "Sort it out yourselves. I'm not getting any more involved."

I nodded my thanks, then turned to look out at the rest of the crowd. Many of them had dispersed toward the grounds, where Garreth now stood next to Sam Montblake. The moon had risen in the dark night, shining its pale white light upon the shifters.

One by one, they began to change. Magic swirled around them, different colors for each person. A moment later, a wolf or mountain lion stood in their place. I even saw a couple of bears and a stag.

With every person that I watched, I felt something spark inside me. A connection of some kind.

When Garreth shifted, I held my breath.

The pale silver light faded from around him, and in his place stood the most glorious black wolf I'd ever seen.

Wow.

"He's something, isn't he?" Kate said.

I nodded mutely, unable to look away.

Midnight Moon 211

"Want to join us for a drink?" she asked.

Yes.

That sounded much better than sneaking into the house to steal the book. But I didn't have a choice.

"Yeah, thanks," I said. "It's a bit cold, so I'm going to go get a sweater. I'd like to check out the beach. Then I'll join you." That should give me ample time to do what I needed to do. Then I'd make a run for it.

"Sure."

I couldn't tell if there was suspicion in her eyes as she watched me walk away, but if there was, she said nothing. Sweat broke out on my skin as I hurried past people gathered around fire pits, sipping waters. I'd at first thought they were drinking gin and tonics or some other clear alcoholic beverage, but I was pretty sure now that it was just water.

These were the guards, meant to protect the main house while the others shifted for the full moon. Garreth might be trying for a peace with the City Pack, but he still didn't trust them.

Or me.

He was smart not to.

Quickly as I could, I hurried into the house. The place was silent as the grave, with an eerie stillness to the air. In the distance, I heard wolves howling.

It should have been scary, but instead, longing ignited in my soul.

Was I really going to do this?

Yes. I had to.

I steeled myself against any doubts and hurried toward Garreth's office. My footsteps were silent, which only made it easier to hear the thundering of my heart. I'd been such an accomplished thief in the past that my nerves were surprising.

But I'd never had so much to lose, back then.

It had been steal or starve. I hadn't had a choice.

I didn't have a choice now, either, but I was risking losing Garreth.

Not that I'd ever had him.

Nor did I really want him—not now that I knew he was planning to erase my memory.

When I reached the office door, I found it shut.

And locked.

Shit.

Double shit.

Hurriedly, I pulled some bobby pins from my pocket. I loathed wearing them for work, but they did come in handy in these situations.

With one ear perked for footsteps, I knelt and got to work. The lock was unusually tricky, and it took me a while to realize that it wasn't going to come undone. Every time I thought I was successful, the thing locked itself again.

Even weirder, I felt the faintest prickle of something against my fingertips as I worked.

Midnight Moon

Was it magic, a spell that kept the lock from being picked?

Could be.

I groaned as I stood. This was already going to be harder than I expected.

I'll be fine.

There was still time left to get the book, and I had a Plan B.

Garreth's office had a patio accessed by large glass doors. It might be on the second level, but that wouldn't stop me.

I shoved the pins back in my pocket and hurried back down the hall. Before I exited the house, I stopped by my temporary room to get a black jacket. It really was chilly outside, and if Kate saw me, I wanted proof that I'd done what I'd said I was going to do. It would also be helpful to have the camouflage while I scaled the outer wall of the house.

As I stepped out onto the main patio, I shrugged into my jacket. Fortunately, Garreth's office faced away from the crowd that was partying, toward the water, where I'd have a good line of sight of any approaching wolves. The woods where they ran were on the other side of the house.

I was getting lucky.

No one looked my way as I headed around the side of the house, going toward the quiet part of the lawn where Garreth's office was located.

In the distance, I heard the waves lapping against the rocky shore, and the sound of wolves howling in the woods. I tuned my hearing toward anything that might be approaching and thanked my lucky stars for my excellent eyesight. Like my hearing, it was unnaturally good by human standards. Now, I knew why. With just the moonlight above, I could see everything as if it were daylight.

When I reached the other side of the house, I checked for anyone who might be nearby.

The coast was clear—literally. Even the boats on the dock were unoccupied, and no one was walking along the water.

I looked up at the massive house. Multiple patios extended from various rooms, and it was difficult to pinpoint exactly which patio was his, but I was pretty sure it was the one closest to me.

I gave my surroundings one last look, then began to climb. The ground floor of the house had unusually high ceilings, so it took longer than it would have on a normal house, nor was it easy to find handholds. Still, I managed, adrenaline driving me onward. Finally, I reached the second level and climbed over the thin metal railings.

Heart pounding, I crouched low near the floor, in case someone looked up, then made my way to the big glass door.

Please be unlocked.

Midnight Moon

I wasn't so lucky, and this wasn't a normal lock that I could pick, either. Worse, the door seemed to spark with magic like the interior lock had. I chewed on my lip.

What the hell was I going to do?

As I stared at the door, the moon drifted across the sky, shining bright light over me. It seeped into my soul, making every atom of my being vibrate. I drew in a deep breath, my head spinning from the strange sensation.

Unable to help myself, I looked up at the moon, entranced by its glorious white glow. It sang a wordless song to me, one that I heard with my bones as much as my ears.

What's happening to me?

It took everything I had to look away from the moon and return my attention to the door. I had to figure this out. Everything was at stake. Three lives. Mine, Meg's, and Garreth's. I couldn't be seduced by the damned moon into forgetting my goal.

But how the hell was I going to get into this office? The glass was incredibly thick and likely enchanted to be extra strong. Even if I could break it, the noise would be super loud.

My mind raced as I sorted through the problem, but I came up with nothing. The moon kept pulling at me, distracting me, and I felt like a character made of silly putty being torn apart by two aggressive children. Frustration buzzed inside my chest, and a low growl of annoyance rose in my throat.

Damn it, there had to be a way.

I clenched my fists, digging my nails into my palms as I struggled to ignore the pull of the moon and tried to figure out how to get through this damned glass.

Suddenly, pain pierced my palms.

I gasped, opening my hands to reveal bloody puncture wounds. My nails had turned into sharp, curved claws.

Holy shit.

I gaped at them in horror.

What the hell was happening to me?

I'm shifting.

19

Lyra

The moon was too damned powerful. It sang to me, its siren song seeping through my veins and muscles, trying to force me to change.

Why now?

Was there something special about this moon?

Or was it my proximity to dozens of other shifters?

Whatever it was, I didn't have time for this. I needed to get that damned book before midnight.

Thankfully, when I caught sight of my reflection in the glass, I still looked like myself. Just my fingernails had changed, shifting into small but deadly sharp claws, claws that sparked with magic.

Why had just my nails transformed, though?

I looked back at the glass, my mind returning to a movie I'd seen a few weeks earlier. A man had used a sharpened piece of metal to carve a circle into some glass, then he'd punched through it.

Had my subconscious remembered that, my body transforming in response?

That would be cool.

I had to try.

Shaking with adrenaline, I raised my hand to the glass and used the claw on my pointer finger to scratch a near-perfect circle into the glass. Magic sparked around my fingertip, little white lights that awed me.

When it was done, I drew my hand back and slammed my palm against the middle of the circle as hard as I could. The glass popped out, landing on the rug inside the office.

Holy tits.

That just happened.

I looked at the glass, then at my claws, shocked.

I have superpowers.

I wanted to keep staring at my claws in awe, but there was no time. I needed to get in and get out.

Carefully, I climbed through the large circle that had been cut into the glass, my footsteps silent on the rug within. Once I was inside, I hurried to the bookshelf where I'd seen the book.

But it was gone.

I stared at it, horror eating at my insides.

Where the hell was it?

Frantic, I raced around the room. The clock showed that there was only an hour until midnight, and if I missed that window, Garreth would pay the price. Then Meg. Then me.

Heart thundering, I checked every bookshelf. I'd never felt so frantic, and the feeling curdled my stomach.

Finally, I finished searching all the shelves and tables, but it was nowhere to be found.

I turned to the massive slab of wood that made up the desk. It wasn't on the surface, but when I went around to the back, I spotted a couple of drawers in the base.

When I tried to open them, only the top one was unlocked. It revealed a boring collection of pens and paper, along with a calculator and some stamps.

The bottom drawer, however, resisted my attempt to open it. I knelt, inspecting the little lock in the drawer. It looked like something I could pick, and even better, I couldn't feel any kind of magical spell on it. I wasn't an expert at it or anything, but it sure didn't feel like the last lock had.

Quick as I could, I pulled the bobby pins out of my pocket and got to work. I was nearly there when I heard footsteps in the hall.

Shit.

Had the lock on this drawer triggered an alarm

when I'd fiddled with it? Was that why I hadn't felt a magic spell?

I could hide under the desk, but the person would surely see me if they walked around it. And then there was the little matter of the gaping hole in the glass that led to the balcony.

Nope, hiding wouldn't work. Instead, I surged to my feet and raced to the door, hiding against the wall so that I could surprise the person when they walked in.

But surprise them with what?

I wasn't much of a fighter.

My gaze landed on a large glass paperweight in the middle of the coffee table. I sprinted to the table and grabbed it, then tucked myself back into my hiding place. My heartbeat nearly deafened me as I waited, hearing the footsteps grow closer.

My hearing was even better than it had been, I realized. Almost as if the skills I needed were developing when I most desperately needed them.

Finally, the person was at the door. The doorknob turned slowly, and I waited, praying that shifters had increased healing capacity like I did. I wasn't superhuman or anything, but I'd always gotten over injuries incredibly quickly.

It was Seth who walked in, and I didn't hesitate.

Before he could turn and see me, I slammed the paperweight against his temple, trying to hit him hard enough to knock him out but not kill him.

Midnight Moon

He collapsed like a bag of rocks, and fear shot through me.

"Seth?" I whispered, dropping to his side and checking his head. It looked okay. And he had a pulse.

Just unconscious.

Thank God.

Shaking, I dropped the paperweight and dragged his belt from its buckle. It took most of my strength to roll his huge form over and pull his hands behind his back, but I managed. Within a minute, I had his hands bound with his belt and his feet tied together with his shoelaces. The final touch was to tear a strip off his shirt and gag him.

Once I had him stashed away near the wall, I hurried back to the desk. The adrenaline was racing so hard through my body that I thought I might be sick, but I tried to use it to help me move faster as I worked at the lock.

Please be in here.

Finally, the lock popped, and I dragged the door open.

Immediately, my gaze landed on the book.

"Oh, thank God." I grabbed it and tucked it inside my jacket, making sure it was wedged into my waistband and out of sight.

Without a backward glance, I ran from the room, shutting the door carefully behind me. I kept my footsteps silent as I went down the hall. Fortunately,

I didn't run into anyone else as I made my way outside.

There were still thirty minutes until midnight, but I didn't want to rejoin the group. I'd surely give myself away with the guilt that had to be written all over my face.

It's just a book.

Valuable, but still just a book. It would be fine.

Instead, I went to the water. I could stand there while I waited to make my way to the meeting place. Surely, people would think I just wanted to enjoy the view. Who wouldn't? It was gorgeous, with the way the water lapped at the shore, the moonlight sparkling on it like diamonds.

I stopped at the edge, the book burning a hole against my skin where it was tucked into the waistband of my jeans. My heart went a mile a minute as I waited for midnight.

Not long now.

I felt him before I heard him.

Garreth.

His presence was like a balm to my soul. If I hadn't heard about his horrible plans, I'd surely be trusting him by now.

It would be my mistake.

Still, my heart raced as I turned to see him. I *wanted* to see him. I was excited to. I ignored the fact that I had the book tucked in my clothes, hoping he wouldn't notice.

No matter what he had planned for me or how much I couldn't trust him, I stupidly wanted this one last moment with him.

He approached slowly, his wolf form enormous and graceful. He'd been the biggest wolf by far, even larger than Montblake. Every inch of him seemed to ripple with muscle, and he prowled with the incredible grace of an apex predator. And yet, his golden eyes weren't vicious as they looked at me. I couldn't tell what the expression was, but it made my heart race faster.

As he drew near, it was easier to see how magnificent he was. The sight of him took my breath away, and my hand shook as I held it out toward him.

He stopped in front of me, letting me place my hand on his head. He was so large that he could probably crush me with his weight if he jumped on me. Not to mention the fangs and claws.

I should be terrified.

Instead, I was awed.

His fur was soft and his eyes beautiful. *All* of him was beautiful. Even more so when he transformed back to human. He wore the same clothes he had before, but I had eyes only for his face. Now that he was human, I could read him better. His expression took my breath away.

There was longing there. I was sure of it.

"Garreth." My voice was soft.

"Lyra." He raised a hand to my face and cupped my cheek.

The heat burned me, but I leaned into his touch, wanting more of it. Tension tightened the air between us, wrapping us up in our own little world.

"You're too dangerous for me," he said, his gaze on my lips.

"I think it's the other way around."

"Perhaps." His voice was rough. Low.

For the briefest moment, I thought he might kiss me, and I had no idea what I would do if he did. There was no way I could kiss him back—not now that I knew he was planning to erase my memory.

And yet, I wanted to.

Stupid.

Instead, he pulled away, backing up slowly.

"You weren't afraid of me," he said.

"That's why you approached? To see if I was afraid?"

He said nothing.

"Well, I'm not."

"Good." He turned, transforming as he spun around. One moment, he was a man. The next, a wolf. He launched himself into a run, so powerful that the sight took my breath away.

He disappeared, and I let out a shuddery breath and turned back to the water.

It was nearly midnight. I had to do this.

Midnight Moon

Fortunately, Garreth had gone the other direction. Montblake had clearly put some thought into his meeting location, and I was grateful. I didn't want to be caught if I could help it, and I was planning to make my way to the garage to get my bike when this was over. After all of this, I couldn't return to my life. I needed to find a life somewhere, and escape would be the first part of that.

Quickly, before I could change my mind, I made my way along the shore to the space where the forest joined the water. When I reached the trees, I turned inland and walked between the massive trunks. The moonlight was scattered by the branches, but I clung to it as I walked. For some reason, I found it comforting.

I reached the clearing too soon.

I'm not ready.

There was no time to dwell on it, however. Within a minute, a massive mountain lion strolled out of the trees. The moonlight glinted on his fur, but my gaze went immediately to his claws and fangs.

Fear shot through me, so different than the awe I'd felt when I'd seen Garreth as a wolf.

They could both kill me in a second, but Montblake would be happy to. Garreth would struggle with it.

Was I making a mistake?

He shifted into his human form, looking just as deadly in his jeans and boots. The coldness in his eyes was enough to freeze the blood in my veins, and I drew in a shuddery breath, trying to get ahold of myself.

"You've got it?" he asked.

"Um. Yeah."

He strode toward me and held out a hand. "Hand it over, and you're free."

"My friend and Garreth, too?"

He nodded.

"I want to see you release my friend."

"I had a feeling you would say that." He pulled his phone from his pocket and typed a few buttons, then turned it toward me. I watched as Meg stepped out of a house in the city, a dazed expression on her face. "We gave her something to erase her memory. She won't remember what happened."

Probably the same thing Garreth had planned to give me. But at least I agreed with this application. "Good."

Montblake took his phone back. "Now the book."

My hand shook as I pulled it from the waistband of my pants, but before I could even hold it out to him, he snatched it from me. As soon as it was out of my possession, guilt exploded within me, worse than anything I'd felt until now.

Why was this book so valuable? It had to be worth more than just a lot of money.

I hesitated, unable to help myself, and reached for the book to take it back, but that was as far as I got.

Midnight Moon

Arms closed around me from behind, yanking me away from him. I didn't recognize whoever had me, which meant it had to be one of his pack.

I kicked and punched, trying to break free. Out of the corner of my eye, I spotted the dark fur of an enormous wolf.

Garreth.

His golden eyes glowed from between the trees.

He'd seen everything

Shit.

"Let me go!" I shouted, trying to kick the person who'd grabbed me.

Ten feet away, Montblake pulled a bag out of thin air and shoved the book inside. A moment later, the bag disappeared.

Garreth lunged from the trees, his powerful form hurtling across the clearing.

He's coming for me.

Somehow, I knew it deep in my soul. Montblake transformed into his mountain lion form and turned on Garreth. As I struggled to break free from my captor, Garreth and Montblake collided in an explosion of claws and fangs. Their growls chilled my soul as they tore at each other.

Garreth landed a vicious bite to Montblake's shoulder, but the mountain lion managed to swipe at his underbelly.

Garreth growled and moved back, his eyes flashing with pain.

Panic flashed through me.

I couldn't let anything happen to him. The instinct exploded inside me, a bone-deep need to protect him.

My mate.

No. He couldn't be. That had to be just a story.

But it didn't matter. I was still desperate to protect him, especially when three other mountain lions prowled from the forest, headed straight to him.

Four against one. It wasn't fair. He couldn't survive that.

I thrashed against my captor, screaming as I tried to break free. But I was too weak.

Desperation rushed through me, wild and fierce. It fueled me, along with the moonlight on my skin. I could feel the light like a brand, and I absorbed it into myself.

As the mountain lions and wolf slammed together in a vicious fight, I felt something happen inside me. Magic sparked through my veins, unmistakable.

Then pain.

Horrific pain.

My bones and muscles tore apart and remade themselves. One moment, I was struggling to break free of my captor. The next, I was on the ground, standing on four unrecognizable feet.

The man who'd been holding me cursed and scrambled back, clearly desperate to get away from me.

Midnight Moon

I ignored him and charged toward Garreth, throwing myself between him and the mountain lions.

They growled and attacked. I slammed into one, going for the throat, and felt my fangs sink into flesh. It was both disgusting and satisfying, and I tore at my enemy. He growled and yanked away, but another lion took his place, swiping at me with massive claws.

All around, a bigger fight broke out. Wolves poured from the forest, colliding with mountain lions. To my left, Garreth fought two. It was a vicious, beautiful battle, but I couldn't take the time to look.

Instead, I chased after Montblake. He was sprinting away from the fight, heading through the woods. Instinct drove me, and I followed him.

Power surged through my veins as I ran, hurtling over fallen logs and boulders, dodging around trees. I'd never felt so alive in my whole life.

I forced myself to run faster, trying to gain on Montblake. But he was too fast. The distance between us increased, and no matter how far I pushed myself, I couldn't close it.

Finally, he disappeared from sight.

I kept running, hoping I would still catch him, but it eventually became clear that I'd lost him.

I slowed, my lungs burning and my chest heaving.

How far had I gone?

Probably miles. I didn't recognize the land around

me, and I was pretty sure I heard cars in the distance. Disappointment surged through me.

I'd definitely lost him. The bastard had probably made it to the road and a car that he'd had stashed.

Why did I care so much? It wasn't like I'd be able to take the book back—not if I wanted Meg to stay free. In the heat of the moment, I'd chased him, but it was probably better I hadn't caught him.

Before I could look at myself and try to figure out what I'd turned into, I heard the rustling of an approaching animal.

Garreth.

I could smell him, and the scent was intoxicating.

And terrifying.

He'd seen me betray him.

I rose and turned, bracing myself.

20

Garreth

I'd found her.

Lyra stood in front of me, magnificent in her animal form.

I hated the fact that I liked how she looked. She was a damned mountain lion, after all. Yet she was beautiful. Her golden fur was sleek and gleaming, her green eyes brilliant in the dark. Her form was massive—the biggest I'd ever seen—and so gracefully powerful that she took my breath away.

I was such a fool.

Just like my father, I'd fallen for a mountain lion. And she'd betrayed me.

I shifted into my human form, careful not to approach too close. I needed time to shift back in case she attacked.

"You're an incredible liar," I said. "I actually believed that you didn't know you were a shifter."

Confusion flashed in her green eyes. She opened her mouth, but no words came out, of course.

"Shift back," I said. "I want to talk to the woman who betrayed me."

She transformed, but the process took a moment. Finally, she stood in front of me.

"Betrayed you?" Anger echoed in her voice. "I was trying to save you. But it's hilarious to hear you talk about betrayal, when you're the one who brought me here to erase my memory."

Guilt flashed through me, but I banished it. "For this very reason. I knew I couldn't trust you, and making you forget you'd ever met us was the kindest thing for you."

"I think I should get to decide if I keep my memories, thank you very much." Rage vibrated in her voice. "I knew I never should have trusted you."

"*You* trust *me*? That's rich." Anger bubbled up inside me, along with betrayal. "You've been trying to steal from me all along."

I'd begun to suspect it today. She'd been too interested in the book on my office shelf, and it was the one I'd had with me in the hotel.

Midnight Moon

She'd been after it all along.

The knowledge had made me finish reading it, and what I'd found had chilled me to the bone. I'd locked it away inside my office, behind protective shields that she shouldn't have been able to break through.

Lyra was a woman of unexpected talents.

"Do you know what was in that book?" I asked, anger vibrating in my voice.

"No."

"It contains a spell that will evict my pack from this land. Kate didn't think it would work, but apparently Montblake thinks it will."

Her jaw dropped and her eyes flashed with doubt. "That can't be right."

"Of course, it is. You know he wants this land. I'd thought I couldn't trust him, but this was worse than I expected. How long have you been working with them?"

"Working with them? Are you crazy?"

"I saw you give him the book. What do you call that?"

"Being blackmailed." Her jaw tightened. "Not that you would care."

"Blackmailed with what?"

Her jaw moved, as if she were debating telling me. I could all but feel the anger and hurt radiating off her, and it didn't make any sense.

"You don't care," she said.

"You're right, I shouldn't. I saw you betray me and then run away."

"I suppose that's what it looked like I was doing, huh?" She laughed bitterly. "What a fool I've been, thinking that I could maybe have a place here."

"Among my pack?"

"It was a brief, stupid thought, all right?"

A short, incredulous laugh escaped me. "Stupid is right. You're a damned mountain lion and you thought you'd join my pack?"

She stiffened, surprise flashing in her eyes. "Mountain lion?"

"Don't play dumb. Of course, you know what you are." The hurt I'd felt when I'd seen her transform had nearly killed me.

I'd suspected her of *something*, but not this. It was too similar to what had happened to my father.

And yet, here I was. Mated to a mountain lion who had betrayed me. Had my line been cursed?

"You don't even want me to try to explain, do you?"

"No, I don't." I couldn't listen to anymore of her lies. Not right now, at least.

"And you have no defense for your plan to erase my memory?"

I shrugged, the anger a toxic sludge in my veins.

She scoffed. "I've been trying to live my life and get by, then I get dragged into your stupid magical world.

And your big plan was to erase my memory and chuck me back out, huh?"

It sounded terrible when she said it like that, but I wouldn't stoop to trying to defend myself to her.

"Montblake left you behind, did he?"

"Of course, he did. I was chasing him."

"Trying to get away, more like."

"Of course, I wanted to get away from you." She shook her head, incredulous. "I knew what you planned."

How naive I'd been, to think that I could erase her memory of me and then watch over her while she lived in the human world. My desire to protect her felt ridiculous now.

"You're a thief." I was satisfied to hear that my voice was cold, hard. "And you'll answer to the council."

Lyra

I never got a chance to get my bike and escape. After Garreth found me in the woods, his pack had joined us. I'd been so outnumbered there was no point in trying to fight my way free.

Now, I found myself in a cell. It had been twenty-four hours since the full moon, and I was still locked up. Someone had pushed food through the door a couple times, but that was the most I'd seen of anyone.

Apparently, this was what happened to shifter thieves.

I should have stuck to human crime. At least then, I'd have gotten a lawyer.

But I'm not human.

I was a damned mountain lion. I'd had no idea. When I'd been fighting, I'd just known that I felt big and powerful. I hadn't taken the time to think about what I might be—I'd been too busy trying to survive and catch Montblake.

Deep in my heart, I'd figured I was a wolf like the Olympia Pack. It's what I'd wanted to be.

And yet, I was a mountain lion.

It only made sense, considering my father had been affiliated with them, somehow. I just hadn't wanted to think it was real.

Damn it.

I rolled over on the shitty bunk and stared at the stone wall. How long would they keep me here? Surely, I'd get a trial of some kind.

By the time I heard footsteps in the hall, it could have been minutes or hours. Time had no meaning in this miserable place.

I rolled over, staring at the door made of iron bars. When Garreth stepped into sight, I sat up, unable to help myself.

"You." My heart raced a mile a minute. "You can't hold me like this forever, you know. I have rights."

"Not here."

Fear iced my heart, and I stood, trying to look more confident than I felt. "That can't be true. You have a council. You have rules."

"We do. And I'll turn you over to them. But you won't like it there any better."

Shit, shit, shit.

I believed him.

Hurt and fear gripped my heart.

"I had started to trust you," he said. There was something in his eyes—some kind of pain—but it was gone so fast I thought I might have imagined it.

"That was stupid," I said. "You can't trust anyone."

"That's how you live your life?"

"Of course. *I'm* not stupid." I shouldn't be hurling insults, but it was the one thing I could do to keep myself from crying. I couldn't bear to break down in front of him. "I know what you do to people who betray you. I was too scared to tell you the truth when I first met you, and then I was in too deep."

"The truth." He scoffed.

"Yes, the truth. Montblake kidnapped my best friend and threatened to kill her. And then he threatened to kill you."

"I'm supposed to believe that?"

"I'm telling the truth, damn it."

"Maybe you are." He pulled a small glass vial from his pocket. "Take this truth potion and tell me again."

I was so pissed that I wanted him to believe me. I shoved my hand through the bars and grabbed it. "I'd be happy to."

Quickly, I swigged it back, realizing at the last minute that maybe I'd gotten ahead of myself.

What if it was poison?

"It's fine," he said. "Not dangerous."

"You can read minds?"

"No, but you looked worried."

"Yeah, because I can't trust you. But if this potion is really what you say it is, then believe my next words. I was trying to save my friend. Trying to save you. And I didn't know what was in the damned book! I thought it was just worth a lot of money."

"Why didn't you just tell me this?"

I laughed wildly. "Just tell you? My father told me stories about you. That you killed someone when you were only seventeen because they betrayed you. And then I heard you talking to Seth and saying you'd kill someone else for lying. Frankly, you sounded like a lunatic to me."

A scowl slashed across his face. "Those are out of context."

"I don't know what context makes killing someone okay."

Midnight Moon

"I was protecting my pack."

"Yeah, yeah." Frankly, I didn't want to hear any more about his pack. "When's my trial? I want to get the hell out of here."

"Soon. In the meantime, I have a lot to think about." He turned to walk away, and I moved toward the door, unable to help myself.

I stopped right in front of the bars, staring at his back.

Quicker than lightning, he turned and gripped me by the shirt, pulling me toward the door. For the briefest moment, he looked like he might kiss me. Desperate desire rushed through me, and I gasped.

He shook his head, clearly disappointed. "I can't believe you're my mate."

"You're joking, right?"

He gave a bitter laugh. "Stop with the games. Of course, you knew."

"I—"

He turned and walked away before I could get the words out.

Heart pounding, I watched him go.

His mate.

Not only was I locked up, but I had a mate. I had to admit that I'd started to suspect it was possible, but hearing it was another thing all together.

How the hell had this become my life? And how was I going to fix it?

. . .

~~~

That's it for *Midnight Moon*! Book two, *Hunter's Moon,* will be here in February. Click here to check it out.

THANK YOU FOR READING!

I hope you enjoyed reading this book as much as I enjoyed writing it. Reviews are *so* helpful to authors. I really appreciate all reviews, both positive and negative. If you want to leave one, you can do so at Amazon or GoodReads.

ACKNOWLEDGMENTS

Thank you, Ben, for everything. There would be no books without you.

Thank you to Jena O'Connor and Lexi George for your excellent editing. The book is immensely better because of you! Thank you to Susie and Aisha for your eagle eye at finding errors.

Thank you to Orina Kafe for the beautiful cover art.

ABOUT LINSEY

Before becoming a writer, Linsey Hall was a nautical archaeologist who studied shipwrecks from Hawaii and the Yukon to the UK and the Mediterranean. She credits fantasy and historical romances with her love of history and her career as an archaeologist. After a decade of tromping around the globe in search of old bits of stuff that people left lying about, she settled down and started penning her own romance novels. Her Dragon's Gift series draws upon her love of history and the paranormal elements that she can't help but include.

COPYRIGHT

This is a work of fiction. All reference to events, persons, and locale are used fictitiously, except where documented in historical record. Names, characters, and places are products of the author's imagination, and any resemblance to actual events, locales, or persons, living or dead, is coincidental.

Copyright 2022 by Linsey Hall

Published by Bonnie Doon Press LLC

All rights reserved, including the right of reproduction in whole or in part in any form, except in instances of quotation used in critical articles or book review. Where such permission is sufficient, the author grants the right to strip any DRM which may be applied to this work.

Linsey@LinseyHall.com
www.LinseyHall.com
https://www.facebook.com/LinseyHallAuthor

Printed in Great Britain
by Amazon